INTO THE
KILLING SEAS

by Michael P. Spradlin

SCHOLASTIC PRESS | NEW YORK

Library of Congress Cataloging-in-Publication Data
Spradlin, Michael P., author.
Into the killing seas / by Michael P. Spradlin.
pages cm
Summary: In 1945 twelve-year-old Patrick and his younger brother Teddy
stowaway on the U.S.S. *Indianapolis* in a desperate attempt to get back to the
Philippines where they last saw their parents, just before the Japanese invasion—
but when the ship is sunk they find themselves clinging to a piece of debris without
food or water, and with hungry sharks circling below.
Includes bibliographical references.
ISBN 978-0-545-72602-3 (hardcover : alk. paper) 1. *Indianapolis* (Cruiser)—
History—Juvenile fiction. 2. World War, 1939-1945—Pacific Area—History—
Juvenile fiction. 3. Survival at sea—Juvenile fiction. 4. Brothers—Juvenile fiction.
5. War stories. [1. *Indianapolis* (Cruiser)—Fiction. 2. World War, 1939-1945—Pacific
Area—Fiction. 3. Survival—Fiction. 4. Brothers—Fiction.] I. Title.
PZ7.S7645In 2015
813.54—dc23
2014026366

12 11 10 9 8 7 6 5 4 3 2   15 16 17 18 19 20/0

Printed in the U.S.A.   23
First printing, July 2015
Designed by Elizabeth Parisi and Steve Ponzo

★

TO THE CAPTAIN AND CREW OF THE
USS *INDIANAPOLIS*.
A GOOD SHIP AND TRUE.

★

He stands next to my hospital bed in a neat, clean white uniform. So bright it hurts my eyes to look at him. The doctor tells me the relentless sun, reflecting off the ocean, might have permanently damaged my vision. Each night and every morning a nurse puts drops in my eyes. It stings. There are rows upon rows of ribbons on his chest. But right now I can't tell what color they are. Like everything else— since they pulled us out of the water—they all look gray to me.

The doctor says, "Patrick? This is Admiral"— something-or-other, I forget his name as soon as I hear it—"and he wants to ask you some questions." He shakes me gently by the shoulder, because I've closed my eyes again, pretending to be asleep. If I could, I'd like to sleep and never wake up. Not die. I don't mean that. Besides, Benny made me promise to live. Benny made me an honorary marine and always said marines never go back on their word.

But I'd like to sleep. For a really long time. Just to rest and dream. Dream about anything else except what happened. I'd like to dream about going to watch the Detroit Tigers at Briggs Stadium and the smell of the fresh-cut grass and the world's best ballpark hot dogs. About playing baseball in the lot just down the street from Most Holy Trinity Church, and how everybody on each team always wanted to play first base, just like Hank Greenberg. I'd dream about dinnertime at our house on Porter Street. We'd sit and pray, and then we'd eat. Dad would tell us about how everyone had to look sharp at the plant that day because Mr. Ford had come through, inspecting the production lines. I'd dream about Christmastime and standing in line at Hudson's department store to see the windows all decorated up with lights and tinsel.

I'd dream about those things. And I wouldn't wake up for a really long time. Because I for darn sure don't feel like answering some admiral's questions.

"What do you remember, son?" he asks me anyway, even though all the nurses say I'm supposed to be resting. I don't like him calling me "son." I'm *not* his son.

Everything. I remember everything. But I keep quiet.

"What can you tell me about that night, Patrick?" he prods me again.

Nothing. Admiral. Sir.

He wasn't there. Not with us, in the water, fighting for our lives. He hasn't earned the right to ask these questions. And it's not because he doesn't deserve answers. It *was* a catastrophe. Benny used to tell me, "We all got jobs to do, pipsqueak. Yours is to mind your P's and Q's and to listen up when Benjamin Franklin Poindexter, Private First Class, United States Marine Corps tells you what's what, *capisce?*" Half the time I never understood Benny. Except when he told me things that really mattered.

I don't know how long I'd been in the hospital—a couple of days, maybe—when I overheard one of the nurses and orderlies talking about what happened. She said it was the worst disaster in naval history.

I'm sure this admiral has a big job to do, sorting it all out. Men died and people are going to want to understand what happened. Why it happened. But I'll bet right now all he really wants to know is what a twelve-year-old kid from Detroit and his ten-year-old brother—who never speaks—were doing right in the middle of it. He won't get a word out of my little brother, Teddy. Right now Teddy's in the bed across from me, buried in layer upon layer of crisp white bedsheets even though the room is stifling. He's turned toward the wall and huddled up into a ball. He rarely moves. The only time he makes any noise is when he's asleep. And even then he only cries and whimpers.

And no one will tell me where Benny is. Not the doctor, not the nurses, not the orderlies. Nobody.

But the admiral isn't interested in any of that. He just wants to know how two kids managed to stow away aboard the USS *Indianapolis*. His back is straight and his hands are hidden behind his back. His pants are creased and his posture so rigid, it makes me ache just looking at him. He isn't going away. So finally, I open my eyes and slowly sit up in my bed and look him in the eye. My back is sore, my hands are bloodied and scarred. He won't get any answers out of me until he answers *my* questions.

"Where is Benny?" I ask the admiral once more.

He doesn't answer. Just prods me again. "Son, what do you remember about that night? When the ship sank?"

Just for a moment I want to tell him. I really do. But I don't want to get Benny in trouble.

He got us on that ship. Thought he was doing us a favor. But that was before the ship went down. And before the sharks came.

You want answers, Mr. Admiral?

You'll have to ask me the right questions.

The question isn't "What do I remember?"

It's "How will I ever forget?"

CHAPTER ONE

STOWAWAYS

★ ★ ★

27 JULY 1945

Benny's plan could be summed up like this: Put us inside a ventilated crate and load it on board the *Indy*. That was it. No secret identities. No trying to pass us off as really small sailors or Philippine princes or anything like that. Benny had cleverly modified the crate to make it as comfortable as possible for us. There was plenty of room inside, and he'd padded the sides with blankets. He'd loaded it with food and water and even a bedpan. But he wasn't thinking only of our comfort. He'd stenciled AMMUNITION on the side of it. "No swabbie will bother it if they think there's a chance they're gonna get their face blowed off, sport. Sailors ain't tough like us marines. About the most dangerous thing them white pants ever handles is a mop." That's what he'd said to us when he showed us how he planned to get us on board.

I remember being miserable inside that wooden box. Yet once we made it aboard, which was no walk in the park, I felt more joy than I had felt in years. For the first time in a long time, it felt as if we might actually be reunited with our parents. Benny had packed enough food into the crate to last long enough to get us to Leyte, and he brought us fresh water every few hours, whenever he went off watch. If the hold was empty and there was no one around, he stood watch so Teddy and I could get out to stretch our legs. He even snuck us into a nearby bathroom, which he called the "head." But it was so hot and humid down there we just spent most of the time sweating.

"Hang in there, little man," he said. "A couple of more days, we'll be in Leyte. It's all going to work out. We just gotta keep it together."

Except for the unrelenting heat and humidity, I was fine. It was Teddy I was worried about. Ever since we first left Manila three and a half years ago, Teddy hadn't spoken. Not a word. He hadn't liked living in the Philippines much. But everything that came after was more than he could handle.

Mr. Henry Ford had sent my dad to Manila to help the Filipinos build an automotive factory. We'd been living there almost a year. Right before the Japanese attacked in 1941, our parents put us on a plane. They were trying to get us to safety, but at the airfield in Manila, Teddy could only whimper. Because there wasn't enough room on the plane for our parents. Only the two of us. And he couldn't imagine going without them.

There was an elderly nun boarding the plane who was very sick, and she was flying to San Francisco. I remember my mother begging her to take Teddy and me with her. I remember it like it was yesterday.

"My oldest—Patrick—he's a good boy, Sister. He's almost nine and he can help take care of you, if you're not feeling well. And Teddy will do whatever my Patrick says," my mother pleaded with her. "We're from Detroit, we go to Most Holy Trinity every Sunday." The nun's name was Sister Felicity, and she agreed to take us with her.

Then I see my mother, holding my face in her hands, demanding that I pay attention to her.

"You listen to me, Patrick, my sweet boy," she said. "You and Teddy are going with Sister Felicity. This plane will eventually get you to San Francisco. We'll wire ahead and have your aunt Maggie pick you up there. You mind your manners and listen to the sister. And take care of Teddy. Promise me you'll take care of Teddy. Can you do that for me? Your dad and I will be on the next plane, right behind you. Do you understand me, Patrick?"

"Yes, ma'am," I said to her.

My dad knelt down in front of me and put his hand on my shoulder.

"It's going to be okay, champ," he said. "We'll be there before you know it. You mind the sister now, okay?"

"I will, Dad. I promise," I said.

My mother hugged me harder than she ever had in her life. Up until then, I'd never seen my dad with tears in his eyes. It was the last time I saw either of them.

Because there was never another plane out of Manila. Before another one could take off, the Japanese

4

invaded the Philippines. And I can't even think about what must have happened there then.

Sister Felicity was nice to us. She tried to distract us with stories and funny jokes as the plane bounced in the air on its way to Guam, where we had to stop to refuel. But the pilot wouldn't take off again, because there were radio reports of Japanese planes in the area. Then we got the news of the attack on Pearl Harbor. And the Philippines. So we stayed on Guam. But a few days later, December 11, 1941, was when the Japanese arrived.

And they weren't coming to have tea and cookies.

They landed on Guam and gunned everyone down. I remember Sister Felicity pulling us from our beds and telling us to run for the jungle. "Run, boys," she said. "We must run! They're coming! Hide in the jungle!" Only there was no way Sister Felicity, as sick as she was, could ever make it to the jungle. We were barely awake as we stumbled out of the house we were staying in. She gave me a pillowcase full of bread and fruit and a jar of water to carry.

We ran toward the underbrush and I could hear shooting and explosions in the streets. The sounds of roaring vehicles and cracking gunshots behind us and Sister Felicity telling us to "Run faster boys! R—!" There was a loud burst of gunfire, and I heard Sister Felicity scream in agony. And then an explosion. It was a Japanese hand grenade. Later, I learned all too well what those grenades sounded like. Sister Felicity didn't scream anymore. Up until then, her cries were the most horrible sounds I'd ever heard. I was pretty sure she was dead. But I couldn't stop to think about it. Machine gun bullets plowed up the ground around us just as we made it to the tree line.

"Don't look back, Teddy!" I yelled at him. "Don't look back! Keep running!"

And we ran through the jungle, until a small band of Chamorro found us. They were natives of Guam, and they knew the jungle like nobody else. And they were kind to us. They took us in and for three years we survived with them. But we moved all the time, never staying in one place long. Sleeping in the dirt, living off the land, constantly on the lookout for Japanese patrols, because they knew we were there, but they couldn't find us. When they got too close to us in the jungle, we'd drift back into a village and mix in with the locals until they gave up looking. Then we'd sneak out to the jungle again. We learned how to stay invisible.

After a couple of years of living like that, the Americans came back and hit Guam like a thunderbolt from Zeus. That's how I imagined it. Before the war, my dad would always read to me at night. I liked the stories from Greek mythology the best. And when the bombs started dropping and the ships started lobbing artillery at the island, this time it was the Japanese who did the screaming.

The Americans retook the island and I thought, *This is it! This is what me and Teddy have been waiting for.* But they wouldn't let us go back to Manila to look for our parents. They said it was because they were still fighting a war. An orphanage opened up and another nun named Sister Mary Teresa came to run it. And that's where they stuck us, until the navy could "figure out what to do with us."

And that's where we first met Benny, a United States marine from the Bronx. He'd been part of the

Guam invasion and was wounded in the fighting. Benny talked and acted like a tough guy. But in truth he was pretty kindhearted. He liked to come by the orphanage while he was healing up from his injuries. Sometimes he brought us comic books he said he didn't have time to read, or a baseball to toss around. And he always had naughty jokes. Lots of them. Sister Mary Teresa would wag her crooked finger at his "salty language," but she could never stay mad at him. Nobody could. Not for long, anyway. There was just something about him. He had an easy way with people. There was always a smile on his face, and he called everybody he met "chum" or "sport" or "ace."

He'd been in combat on islands all around the Pacific. According to him, he'd been kicking the—I couldn't say the word or Sister Mary Teresa would get really mad, but it rhymed with "wrap"—out of the Japanese. "Chasing their little Imperial butts all the way back to Tokyo" is what he said. By the time he snuck us aboard the ship, Benny had recovered from his wounds and had been training with a battalion of marines for the invasion of Japan. That was the next step, everyone said. If they didn't surrender, the Americans were going to invade the Japanese homeland. Benny said he'd "walk right into Hirohito's palace, snatch him up by his collar, and teach him a thing or two about a thing or two." Hirohito was the emperor of Japan and judging by the way Benny talked about him, he was clearly not one of Benny's favorite people.

But me and Teddy were. Benny looked out for us. Said we reminded him of the stoop boys back home in the Morris Heights section of the Bronx, where he grew up. And I don't know how he did it, but eventually he "talked to a sergeant who knew a sergeant that owed another sergeant a favor" and got his orders changed. Now he was assigned to the marine detachment aboard the USS *Indianapolis*. "Always remember it's the sergeants that runs all of your military units, pipsqueak. Don't never ask no officer if you need somethin'. Your average officer couldn't find his hind end with a both hands and a map."

It was July of 1945, and the *Indy* was heading for the

Philippines. Back toward Manila where our parents were. And Benny had a plan. Because like he said, "No bunch of white-suited, lamebrained, mop-drivin' swabbies is gonna keep two red-blooded American boys away from their parents or by all the saints in heaven, my name isn't Benjamin Franklin Poindexter, Private First Class, United States Marine Corps. If the United States Navy is gonna keep you two kids from findin' your parents, what the heck are we over here fightin' for?" Only he didn't say heck. He said a bad word that rhymed with "smell." But I didn't care about that. Because Benny planned a pretty brilliant way to sneak us aboard.

That's how we got on the ship. How we ended up packed in a crate with Teddy whimpering in the heat and me counting the minutes until we'd land in Leyte. It wasn't Manila, but at least it was the Philippines.

Teddy didn't like being in the crate or the darkness of the hold or even leaving Guam. Down there in the hot, sweaty gloom I thought about it a lot. Maybe I should have left him at the orphanage with Sister Mary Teresa and gone to Manila by myself. Once I found Mom and Dad, I could bring them back to Guam and we'd all be together again.

"How will we get from Leyte to Manila, Benny?" I'd asked him when he'd told me his plan for our "free ride" aboard the USS *Indianapolis*.

"Don't worry about that, chum," Benny said. "We do it a step at a time. We get you to Leyte first, and then we'll worry about getting you to Manila. Heck, even if we get caught in Leyte, it'll be easier for the navy to ship you on to Manila than all the way back to Guam."

With Benny's help, we got in the crate at the ammo depot at twilight on the twenty-seventh. He had it loaded onto a launch and with a sailor at the helm, piloted it out to the *Indianapolis*, which was bobbing gently at anchor in the harbor. Everything went surprisingly smoothly, until the crate actually sat down on the ship's deck.

That's when the trouble started.

CHAPTER TWO

IN THE BELLY OF THE BEAST

★ ★ ★

28 JULY 1945 – 29 JULY 1945

Trouble came in the form of another marine named Stenkevitz. He was a sergeant, and right away, I could tell by his voice that he didn't like Benny.

"Where you going with that crate, private?" he barked. A crane had lifted the crate onto the deck, and from there Benny had wrestled it onto a cart. He was wheeling it across the deck to stow it in the hold belowdecks, when he was intercepted by Stenkevitz.

"Sarge, all I know is the captain wants extra twenty-millimeter ammo laid in. We're supposed to be doing a gunnery exercise when we arrive in Leyte," I heard Benny say. The support boards that crisscrossed the crate on the outside had small spacers inserted in between them and the wooden sides. It allowed plenty of air inside and just enough of a gap for me to peer out and see what was happening, but you'd never notice them unless you were looking really close. And like Benny said, no swabbie wanted to get close to a box full of what they thought was live ammunition.

Stenkevitz was a short, squat, barrel-chested man with a thick brow and huge arms. I could see his face well enough through the small crack. He had unfriendly eyes. And even though he was clean-shaven, he had thick whiskers shadowing his face.

"Then why aren't you taking it to the armory with the rest of the ammo? If we get attacked by genuine Japanese planes along the way, won't it be handier in the armory?" Stenkevitz challenged him.

Benny had a ready answer. "I'm not sure, Sergeant. But I was taught to think like a marine on my first day of basic training, so I suspect there's a couple of reasons the cap'n ordered it taken to the hold. First, we're takin' this here ship straight to Manila and seeing as Hirohito and Tojo and all the rest of their buddies is just about done in, they probably ain't got any planes left to fly this far south. If we see one, we might as well surrender. Second, if you read the orders, Sarge, you'll see the part about the gunnery exercise. It says, 'live ammo training upon arrival.' Now I ain't never served on the *Indy*, because I for sure ain't one of the corps' finest like you is, Sarge. But I hear Captain McVay is one heck of an officer, for a mop driver, and got them railroad tracks on his collar for a reason. Since we're gonna shoot off the guns before we get to Leyte, that probably means we're gonna need some extra bullets. Which makes it likely this crate and probably several more like it has gotta be stored in the hold, because the armory is full of the ammo we'll need if the ship is actually attacked. But I'm only a private, not a sergeant like you. So I'm just guessing."

Stenkevitz was quiet for a moment. He knew he'd been insulted by Benny, but he wasn't quite clever enough to figure out how. He locked his hands together, cracked his knuckles, and decided to get tough.

"Are you trying to get smart with me, private?" Stenkevitz scowled, walking right up to Benny and sticking his nose in his face. This sergeant looked like a hard man and mean as a snake. It was almost like he

14

wanted to fight. I hoped he wouldn't hurt Benny. I'd seen a lot of fights between sailors and marines on Guam after the Americans retook the island. They could beat each other up pretty bad. Sister Mary Teresa said it was because they couldn't "hold their liquor." She said they'd been fighting their way through the Pacific and that built up a lot of stress. "And they are men, after all," she'd say, and roll her eyes. As if that explained everything.

"No, Sarge. I'm already smart," Benny said. "I'm just relayin' the cap'n's orders is all. But if you have a problem with it, I'll be more'n happy to run up to the bridge and ask him where he wants me to park this here crate. I can stash it anywhere, the galley, the gedunk, your quarters, wherever you want it, Sarge, just say the word."

"Maybe I should inspect the contents of that crate. Make sure you aren't smuggling hooch or contraband on board a US Navy vessel."

"Be my guest, Sarge. I'm sure it won't happen again. And I'm sure the captain won't mind."

Stenkevitz paused, confused. I was sweating now, and not just because of the heat and humidity. If

Stenkevitz found us in the crate, he would turn us in and Benny would be in a lot of trouble. Probably they'd lock him up in the brig. At the orphanage, Benny had told us he'd spent a fair amount of time in the brig, himself.

"What isn't happening? The captain ... what are you talking about, Poindexter?" he demanded. And then he called Benny a bad word. He was lucky Sister Mary Teresa wasn't around.

"I'm just sayin' I heard from Gunny Franklin in the ammo depot on Guam that the captain was in a big hurry to get underway. Apparently there's a lotta new crew coming on board and they're green and he wants to get in some gunnery training before we put in at Leyte. Word is, the *Indy* is going straight on to Japan after the Philippines. Gonna sail right up to Hirohito's palace and turn it into an outhouse. So I got this crate and three more like it I gotta get stowed in the hold. You wanna inspect them, be my guest. I'll just wait until you're done. I could use a smoke. On second thought, I most likely ain't gonna smoke, because I've seen some real bad things happen when someone forgets and grabs a cigarette around live ammo. All I ask is *you* tell the captain why we was late getting the extra ammo stowed away. I don't wanna get in no trouble, Sarge." Benny hooked his thumbs in the web belt of his khaki pants waiting for the slow-witted sergeant to make up his mind.

Stenkevitz stood there rubbing his chin with his ham-sized hand. Finally he just snarled at Benny, "Get moving, private. And stay out of my hair. I mean this whole voyage. I don't like you, Poindexter, you pig-faced sack of dung. You even look at me cross-eyed, I'll have you thrown in the brig. You hear me, marine?"

"Loud and clear, Sergeant. Wouldn't have it any other way," Benny said cheerfully as he grabbed the cart handle and pulled it across the deck. Stenkevitz must have moved off to torment someone else, because I could no longer see him.

"Guy couldn't spell 'cat' if you spotted him the C and the T," Benny whispered to us through the crate. "And what a horrible poker player. Owes me three hundred bucks, thinks I'll forget about it because of those stripes on his sleeve. But Benny Poindexter, Private First Class,

United States Marine Corps don't forget nothin'. You okay in there, Patty boy? What's the signal?"

I rapped on the lid of the crate with my knuckles rapidly twice, then once a few beats later. That was our secret sign. In case Benny ever came to check on us, but somebody else was in the hold, he'd knock and let us know it was safe to come out. "But don't worry, anybody coming down to the hold don't hang around long. It's too dang hot. And seeing how this crate is marked, ain't nobody gonna touch it unless they absolutely have to. Them swabbies don't know which end of a gun to point at the enemy anyway. It's all they can do just to steer this bucket of bolts."

We made it safely to the hold. And that's where we stayed, following Benny's instructions. He brought us fresh water three or four times the first day, whenever he wasn't on duty. It was unbelievably hot and humid. There were times I thought we'd made a horrible mistake. That we'd never be able to stand the heat another minute and would have to crawl out of the crate where someone would discover us. Sweat soaked through our clothes. The air was still and motionless in the hold. At times, Teddy would curl up into a ball and whimper and I'd have to scurry across the crate and sit next to him, whispering and pleading with him to be quiet so no one would hear us.

"I'm real sorry about the weather, boys, but we're about right smack dab on the equator, and that old sun ain't going to cool off anytime soon. But only a couple of more days and we'll be there. You'll see," he said once, when he brought us water. Benny always had something positive to say. He did his best to keep our spirits up.

At night it was even worse. The temperature dropped, but the humidity rose, and we sweated even more. To make it even more unbearable, the sea grew rougher after sundown and the ship rocked to and fro in the waves. I thought I was going to puke several times. Teddy actually did. Twice. But I couldn't let him out of the crate. If he threw up on deck, someone might discover it. The crate was only about six feet by six feet by four feet, and the smell was awful. I knew he couldn't help it. He was scared. I was scared, too. But honestly, part of me was getting tired of always taking care of him.

He wouldn't talk—not since we left Manila—and he cried all the time. When he didn't cry, he moaned. I had to drag him everywhere. Force him to eat even when he wasn't hungry, and soothe the nightmares that filled his head every evening. Mom made me promise to take care of him. Benny always told me marines don't ever break a promise, and he'd made me an honorary marine. Once, on Guam, when Benny was visiting the orphanage, he heard me snap at Teddy after Teddy threw the baseball through the window. He was always messing up and breaking things, and I guess I'd just had enough that day. Benny took me aside and gave me one of his lectures.

"Hey, champ," he said. "Ease up on the guy. A little brother needs a big brother to watch out for him. Keep him on the straight and narrow. Because let me tell you somethin'. He ain't always gonna be this little. Before you know it, you two are gonna be full-grown men. And then someday you might find yourself in a scrap, and who you gonna look for to have your back? It ain't gonna be the pipsqueak you think of as little Teddy right now. It'll be big Teddy. And when he's full grown, he ain't never gonna forget how his older brother took care of him in the absolute worst time of his life, and he's gonna say to the whole world, 'Anybody wants a piece of my brother, he's gonna have to come through me.' And trust me, sport, you're gonna be grateful he's there backin' you up. Poor little Teddy is just havin' a tough time now. You gotta stick by him. Marines stick together. And we don't never leave no man behind."

I tried not to be mad at Teddy, but it was so hard sometimes with him whining and whimpering and never talking and puking his guts out. I don't know why he never spoke. Teddy was always a little nervous and jerky, even back in Detroit. He was just a little over six years old when we left Mom and Dad in the Philippines. I guess somewhere deep inside he must have realized what was happening, that we might not see them again. And he couldn't take the thought of it. Sister Mary Teresa said that Teddy was in there. Just that he retreated way down deep inside himself. Anyway, that day after Benny told me to ease up on Teddy, I tried. But it was hard.

Now the ship was rising and dipping like the Thunderbolt, a roller coaster at the Bob-Lo Island amusement park back home. The up and down motion made me feel like I was going to lose it myself. Just when I thought I couldn't take it anymore, I heard Benny rap on the lid of the crate. Two quick knocks, then a slow one. That was the signal that said it was all clear to come out of the crate.

But before he could lift the lid off, light filled the hold, bursting through the small air vents in the sides. And I heard Sergeant Stenkevitz's voice.

"What are you doing down here, Poindexter?" he said.

"Just taking a break is all, Sarge, that's all. And makin' sure I stayed out of your way, like you ordered," Benny said.

"Uh-huh. Why don't you tell me what you got in that crate, private?"

"I told you, Sarge, there ain't nothin' in these crates but shells for them twenties, you want to see? I don't mind—"

Benny never got to finish his sentence.

He was cut off by the loudest explosion I'd ever heard.

CHAPTER THREE

CHAOS

★ ★ ★

The noise thundered like the very metal of the ship was begging for its life. Me and Teddy were jerked off our feet, and our heads banged into each other inside the crate. I sat up stunned, my skull aching, and had to clap my hand over Teddy's mouth to make sure he didn't cry out. Not when Benny'd just about distracted that bully. But it probably wouldn't have mattered anyway. My ears buzzed and it was hard to hear. The lights went out and Sergeant Stenkevitz shouted, "We're under attack! Battle stations!" He kept shouting it over and over as he ran from the hold and his voice faded. A few seconds later another explosion staggered the great vessel. Teddy and I were slammed hard against the side of the crate.

"All right, Patrick, Teddy, listen up. You boys stay right here. I gotta go find out what's happened! We mighta hit a mine, the boiler in the engine room coulda blown, or we could be under attack. I doubt it, but your Japanese Imperial Navy is sneaky by nature and you never know. We left Guam without a destroyer escort, so it could be a sub. Either way, I'll find out what's goin' on. And I'll come back for you. I promise. Do you hear me?"

I was terrified and couldn't think of anything to do except knock on the lid of the crate.

"No! Let me hear you say it, Patty boy. You'll stay here. I'll come back. If for some reason I don't, if you think it's going bad, you get out and get topside and turn yourself in to the first officer you see. Got it?"

I was petrified. I felt like Teddy, like I couldn't speak.

"Patrick James O'Donnell! You got it?" Benny yelled. "Answer me!"

"I got it. I got it, Benny. But please don't leave us, Benny! Benny! Please!"

"I ain't leavin' you, I promise. And Benjamin Franklin Poindexter, Private First Class, United States Marine

Corps don't break a promise. I'm just doin' a little recon is all."

I wanted to believe him, to tell him I trusted him, but I couldn't focus on what he was saying. There was too much noise, and the explosion had left me disoriented and woozy. Everyone aboard that ship was shouting and screaming. I could hear them even though we were way down in the hold. And while I didn't hear Benny leave, I knew he was no longer there. Teddy curled up in a ball in the corner and started making the "ahh ahh" sound he always made when he was terrified. I didn't know how long Benny had been gone, but it seemed like it was quite a while. I couldn't stand it any longer. I pushed the lid of the crate up and peered outside.

It was hard to see in the dark, but Benny had given us a flashlight and I flipped it on. There was smoke pouring into the hold. Pipes had burst and water was shooting everywhere. The floor of the hold was filling with water, and most of the crates and other cargo had rolled all over the floor like dice. Smoke filled the air, making it harder to see by the second. The ship lurched suddenly and threw me off balance. But this time I stood up and pushed the lid of the crate all the way off, grabbed a canteen of water, and clipped it to my belt. I had to see what was going on, what we'd gotten ourselves into.

I could hear men shouting everywhere above us. Their voices sounded scared and desperate, like the ship was in serious trouble. And Benny still hadn't returned. If something had happened to him . . . well, I didn't want to think about it. I wasn't sure what we'd do without him. We'd been banking on his plan, and without him, nothing made sense. I wiped my eyes trying to clear them, and my fingers came away wet. I hadn't realized I was crying. I had counted on Benny. What if he'd been hurt? What would I do now? Teddy yanked on my arm. He was hysterical, wailing and screaming like a banshee. It brought me back to the present. I knew we couldn't just sit there and wait any longer.

"C'mon on, Teddy," I said. "We need to get out of here." I coughed, because the smoke was growing thicker. Teddy wouldn't move from the crate.

"Aah, aah!" he cried. I tried to grab him, but he wriggled away from me. He was shaking, and when I held my hand out to him, I realized that I was, too.

"Teddy! Quit screwin' around," I shouted at him. "We need to get—"

"Patrick!" I heard Benny shout. He'd come back! Just like he promised! But when I turned around to face him I nearly fainted. It wasn't the Benny I recognized.

His face and hands were horribly burned. There were strips of skin hanging from his cheeks and chin, and his hands were curled into ugly, blackened masses.

"Benny!" I cried. "What happened? You're hurt!"

"Just a scratch, sport," he croaked. Something was wrong with his voice. It sounded like he'd swallowed broken glass.

"What do we do, Benny?" I asked. Teddy stood next to me, terrified and clutching at my arm. With each passing second, the smoke in the hold grew thicker.

"Benny," I prodded him. "Tell us what to do."

"We . . . gotta . . ." He sank to his knees. The thunderous groaning sound of metal bending and twisting roared through the air. The ship lurched to the side again, and Teddy and I nearly crashed into Benny, trying to keep our feet. Another pipe burst and water spurted everywhere, soaking us. Teddy and I hacked as the smoke filled our lungs. We could barely see, and it was almost impossible to breathe.

"All . . . right . . . boys," Benny said, wheezing. "Get down on your hands and knees; we're gonna make our way up to the deck. Come on now, you gotta get down low, where the air is clearer."

I did as he instructed and pulled Teddy down beside me. We started crawling toward the main hatch to the hold. Benny crept along behind us. He groaned in agony with nearly every movement he made, but that didn't stop him from encouraging us. "Keep going, boys; stay low!"

I glanced over my shoulder. Crawling was killing Benny. He couldn't use his hands very well, and with every grimace, every jerky inch of progress, I could tell he was in horrible pain. I scrambled back to help, but he wouldn't let me lay a finger on him.

"Don't you worry about me, pipsqueak," he said.

"You and Teddy get to that hatch, then climb up to that deck. That's an order. Do you hear me, marine?"

"Marines stick together," I told him, ignoring his command. "Put your hands and arms up on my back."

"No! No. I can do it. I'll be right behind you, Patty. I swear it." Benny's force of will was staggering as he propelled himself forward. He groaned with every movement, but slowly we made our way through the dense cloud of smoke and the rising water that covered the floor, until we reached the entrance to the hold.

"Good thing for us Stenkevitz didn't dog this hatch, or we'd be stuck," Benny said. I knew from listening to the sailors and marines back on Guam that "dogging the hatch" meant the hatch was shut and sealed tight. Sometimes when ships were hit by enemy fire, the hatches on the entire ship were closed to prevent air from escaping. It helped the vessel stay afloat longer. And sometimes the hatches were sealed with men still inside.

Teddy reached the entrance to the hold first. The passageway outside was smokier and even louder with the noise of running, shouting men. He turned around, staring at me, his eyes wild with fright.

"Okay," Benny croaked. "We're going up to the deck. Be careful, because there are fires everywhere. And you boys don't want to end up lookin' fried like old Benny here, right? Let's go!" Benny staggered to his feet and we began climbing the steps. On every level of the ship, we saw dozens of horribly wounded men crying and begging for help. Some of them were trapped beneath wreckage, unable to move. Able-bodied sailors and marines buzzed about, trying to free them. Some of those men were hurt and bleeding themselves, but they were doing everything they could to assist their shipmates. I saw one sailor pick another up off the deck and throw him across his shoulder. The wounded seaman screamed in agony, but the sailor yelled at him.

"Steady, buddy. Steady, boy," the sailor said. "I got you. I'm getting you topside, and the doc will fix you right up." His friend didn't hear him because he'd passed out.

Everyone who'd been in the bowels of the ship before the explosions was headed upward. The ladders and passageways grew crowded, every man desperate to reach the main deck. As we climbed, I saw a huge, gaping hole in the bulkhead amidships. How had it gotten there? It was gigantic. The ship must have been torpedoed. I couldn't believe a boiler explosion would tear through steel quite like that. But I didn't have time to think about it too carefully. We had to keep moving.

There were times I was certain Benny wasn't going to make it. He would climb a ways, then stop and groan in agony. His cheeks were burned so badly I could see the bone sticking up through the skin and his fingers were curled into useless, charred stumps. He had to hook the rungs on the ladder with his wrists to hold on.

"A little farther, now. We're almost there," he said, breathing hard. "Then we'll find out what's going on. I'm sure they've already radioed for help and rescue ships are on their way. In the meantime, if we gotta abandon ship, we'll find us a life raft. It'll be fine, boys. You'll see."

But it wasn't fine. When we finally reached the main deck, we stepped directly into an inferno. I thought we'd get a little relief from the smoke now that we were in the open, but the air was still heavy with it. It burned my throat and made my eyes sting. But I could see better now. Everything was on fire. I didn't know it was possible for steel to burn, but the deck of the ship was melting right in front of us. The worst part was the scalded, broken seamen who were gathered on the deck. Many of them were horribly injured. They screamed in agony. And those who weren't hurt tried to outyell their suffering comrades. I heard them shouting at the wounded to calm down. That everything would be all right. The medics were going to be here soon.

"Had to be torpedoes," Benny said. "Ain't no boiler or mine woulda done this much damage. Lousy, stinkin' . . ." He went on to call the Japanese all kinds of names. Sister Mary Teresa would have blushed.

Teddy was holding on to my arm, squeezing it so hard it hurt. Benny didn't look like he was going to live through the next five minutes. The smoke was thickening and the fire growing closer; we tried to back up to get free of the flames and smoke, but the deck was crowded with bodies at our feet and wounded men staggering between them, wailing for help they couldn't seem to find. There was no place for us to go. Every couple of seconds, more men appeared on deck carrying injured shipmates. They'd lay them gently on the deck, and someone would try to perform first aid on them.

But I think it was too late for many of them. I'd seen a lot of dead bodies on Guam. The Chamorro killed many Japanese soldiers, who did their own share of killing. I knew what a dead person looked like. Right then, I understood that a lot of the men lying on the *Indianapolis*'s deck were already gone.

Benny realized what we were seeing and sought to shield us from it. "Don't look, boys. Don't look at nothin'. We're going to make our way to the stern. If we gotta abandon ship, we'll get us a raft and go off the ship aft, you understand me?" But I wasn't paying attention to Benny. I was watching the ship fall apart in front of my eyes. I witnessed incredible bravery as sailors and marines did whatever they could to save the *Indianapolis* and each other.

"Listen up, pipsqueak—" Benny's words were cut off as the ship listed sharply. It tilted so severely that it knocked us off our feet and we careened across the deck. The wounded screamed as they slid along the steel surface. Body after body plummeted over the side, splashing into the ocean.

"Hang on! Grab something! Anything! Hold on, boys!" Benny shouted.

Benny managed to wrap his arm around a pipe at the elbow and stop himself from tumbling across the deck, but Teddy and I weren't quick enough and slid toward the side of the ship. I reached out, grabbing my brother by the ankle. With my free hand, I dug my fingernails into the deck, looking for anything I could hold on to. I glanced up and saw to my horror that we were only a few feet from edge, sliding faster with every second.

And in the blink of an eye, Teddy slipped over the side.

CHAPTER FOUR

DESPERATION

★ ★ ★

All I could think about were Teddy's cries as he tumbled through the air. And then I realized he was going to yank me in with him.

"The lifeline, Patrick! The lifeline!" I heard Benny shouting at me. His voice sounded so far away. "Grab hold, little man! Benny's coming!"

The lifeline was a thick rope fence that circled the ship. It ran through a series of stanchions welded to the deck. Its name said it all: It was a last barrier to keep sailors from plunging over the side of the ship in rough seas.

I still gripped Teddy tightly by the ankle, but he was dragging me along with him. Teddy was only two years younger than me, but nearly the same size and weight. I was pretty sure I couldn't hold him.

But once again, I listened to Benny.

"Aah!" Teddy cried as I reached out and snatched hold of the lifeline. I hoped it was still intact. The fire could have burned through it or it could have come apart in the explosion. But luckily for us, it held fast. I gripped the rope with all my strength as I flipped over the side of the ship. I thought my shoulder would be ripped from the socket when Teddy and I finally jerked to a stop. We dangled in the air, Teddy swinging back and forth in my hand.

"Aggh! Benny! Help me! Please! Someone help!" I shouted. I had Teddy tightly around the ankle, but knew I couldn't hold him for long. And I wouldn't have anywhere near the strength to pull him back up. As it was, it was all I could do to grasp the lifeline. We were going to fall into the roiling ocean. Though I could hear the shouting and running of other crewmen above me, no one came to our aid. No one except Benny.

"Hang on, pipsqueak! I'm almost there!" Benny yelled over the chaos. And then he was. His scarred and burned face appeared, staring down at me over the edge.

"Hold on!" he shouted.

"Hurry, Benny! I can't hold him much longer!"

"Aaahh!" Teddy was wailing at the top of his very loud and substantial lungs.

"Almost there, kiddo," Benny croaked. Teddy was slowly slipping from my grip. Benny looked like he could barely move, but somehow he knew we needed his strength.

"Benny! Hurry!" I pleaded with him.

He couldn't use his hands, so he humped forward on his knees and elbows, and leaned over the side.

"All right, kiddo," he said. "You need to listen to me. I'd grab you if I could, but this body of mine ain't workin' like I want it to. So you're gonna swing your leg up and hook it over the lifeline. You're gonna pull the both of you up, understand?"

I thought Benny was crazy. I didn't have the ability to hold us, let alone save us. I was terrified.

"Benny! No! I can't! I'll fa—"

"Listen to me, Patty boy!" he shouted, interrupting me. "This is the only way. Now swing your leg up and hook this rope with it. That's an order, marine!"

I could barely breathe with the strain. But what choice did I have? It took a couple of tries, but somehow I willed my body to cooperate.

"That's it, Patrick," Benny said. "Now comes the hard part. On the count of three, you gotta let go of the rope and grab your brother with both hands. You're safe. You're holding on with your leg. Now take both hands and pull him up on this deck. Do you hear me?"

I couldn't focus. All around me, men cried out in agony, begging for help, for relief from the pain they were feeling. My shoulder was on fire from the strain of Teddy's weight. He was wiggling and thrashing and it was all I could do to keep from dropping him. The strange thing was, the ship was still churning through the water. Either the engines hadn't been turned off, or there was no one left alive in the engine room to shut them down. Just moments ago, I had seen the huge, gaping maw in the middle of the ship. The great vessel was sucking in water. The seawater was taking it down fast. This was the most horrible nightmare I could imagine. Why didn't someone turn off the engines until they figured out what to do?

"Teddy! Teddy!" I shouted, coming back to the moment. "Hold still!" I groaned as my shoulder stretched and my hand cramped. I couldn't drop him. I would never forgive myself.

But Benny was ordering me to do something I was petrified to even attempt. I closed my eyes and saw my mother's face. I could see her standing there at the airfield, tears forming in her eyes as the plane's engines hummed in the background. It was so loud she had to shout to be heard. But she'd told me, "Take care of your brother." I knew she was depending on me.

I glanced up at Benny's burned and disfigured face. Even through the scarred skin I could see the determination in his eyes.

"Okay, Benny," I said. "I'll do it."

Benny counted. "One. Two. Three!"

I let go of the lifeline and grabbed Teddy's leg with my free hand. Teddy swung in my hands and banged hard against the hull of the ship.

"Aaah!" he cried.

"It's okay, Teddy," Benny yelled to him. "We got you. You're safe now."

I heard Benny groan. He had to have been suffering horribly. He was yelling words that, if Sister Mary Teresa had heard him say them, he'd be in trouble for years. He wasn't going to be able to help us. I looked down and saw the ocean waves crashing against the side of the ship. If I didn't do something soon, Teddy and I were dead.

"Benny!" I begged through gritted teeth. "I can't hold him much longer."

"We gotta get him to help," Benny said from above. "The best way you can take care of Teddy is to get him moving."

"Teddy!" I cried. "Teddy, listen to me. You gotta climb up me."

Like always, Teddy didn't answer. He just kept on wailing.

"I know you're scared," I pleaded. "I am, too. But you have to do this. I'm going to swing you, and you have to reach up, grab me, and climb back up onto the deck. For Mom and Dad. You have to!"

He didn't want to do it. I know he didn't. But when I started swinging us both back and forth, he let out a big scream and lurched upward, grabbing onto my waist. We wriggled in the air like two earthworms on a fishhook. "You can do it, buddy," I whispered. I was trying to be like Benny. Positive. Encouraging. "I know you can. You have to."

And slowly, Teddy pulled himself up. Inch by inch he rose back toward the deck and scrabbled over the side.

Now it was my turn. I was tired. So tired. But Teddy had done something I never thought he'd be able to, because we had no other choice. Maybe I could, too.

"Almost there, buddy!" Benny shouted. "You gotta do it. You done good and now you gotta finish the job. Pull! Come on now! Pull!" I pulled and strained every muscle in my body, and with one final effort, I swung my torso up, got a hand on the lifeline, and yanked myself up onto the deck. Teddy quickly crawled away from the edge and huddled against my side, sobbing. The three of us sprawled, exhausted, on our backs. We paused only long enough to take hold of the lifeline. I pried Teddy's arm from around my chest and placed his hand on the rope, closing mine over his.

"It's okay now, Teddy," I said softly. "You're okay now."

The ship was still listed at a very sharp angle, and if it tilted any farther, we could easily plunge into the sea all over again. As we lay there, the heat from the deck penetrated through my shirt, reminding me that the ship was going up in flames.

"Come on, boys," Benny said. "We can't stay here. I ain't heard no order yet, but I bet you a piece of Lindy's cheesecake—the best slice in New York City—we gotta abandon ship. This tub is gonna sink."

Just then, as if to reinforce Benny's point, the ship cracked with a loud snapping noise and the gap amidships opened wider. All around us, men were losing their footing, somersaulting down the deck, and plunging into the sea.

"Okay, Patty boy!" Benny croaked, his voice sounding weaker and worse by the minute. "We can't crawl all the way to the stern. We'll never make it. Everyone hold on to that lifeline and don't let go of it for nothin'."

Somehow he staggered to his feet. We all grabbed on to the rope and lurched single file along the edge of the deck, dodging sailors, flames, and burning debris, as we made our way to the stern.

When we arrived there we found hundreds of men gathered at the ship's railing. Some of them wore life jackets and some didn't, but everyone wanted one. It was mass confusion. Two sailors had a net full of life jackets they poured onto the deck. There was a mad dash to get them. We were too far away through the crush of bodies to reach any. Especially since the men weren't being too polite about it. Fists were flying right and left. And once they'd gotten their hands on a vest, some of the men were jumping straight into the water. A couple of young officers stood at the stern with their hands up, shouting and pleading with the men to stay on board. That help had to be on the way.

"There has been no order to abandon ship!" one of them shouted. "Wait until we receive instructions." But no one was really paying attention. Some of the men were even jumping into the water without life vests. This was what desperation looked like.

I was terrified at the thought of abandoning ship. I

wasn't a good swimmer, and I didn't want to jump into the ocean.

"Benny!" I yelled over the noise. "Can't we just stay on board? Somebody's got to be here soon to rescue us, right? Like the officers said. Can't we wait?"

Benny shook his head. "I don't think so, sport," he said. "I'm sure there's ships and planes on the way right now, but I don't think the *Indy* is gonna last until they get here. We gotta find us some life jackets and a raft.

"Hey, you! Sailor," Benny hollered to a man standing in front of him. "Where can we get some life jackets?"

The man didn't respond.

I reached out and tapped him on the shoulder. The man turned and looked at us, and saw three miserable saps: I was exhausted and Teddy still whimpered. In that moment, we probably looked a whole lot younger than we were. And Benny's face was horribly burned and disfigured. The sailor's eyes widened in surprise. He sucked in a hissing breath and backed away from us into the crowd.

"Cripes," Benny said, watching the man push himself through the crowd as if he'd just seen a ghost. "Tell me true, Patty boy. Do I look that bad?"

Even then, I couldn't lie to Benny. "You look pretty bad. It's just burns, though. I'm sure you're going to be fine, once we get you to a doctor." Maybe that was a little bit of an exaggeration. Benny looked horrible. And I was worried about him, because he seemed to be weakening.

I'd spent the last few years of my life watching people die in all kinds of ways. I'd seen wounded Chamorro guerrillas in the jungle that would come back hurt from a fight and slowly waste away from their injuries. American soldiers shot down by the Japanese. All around me had been war, death, and chaos, and I knew what it was like to watch someone die. Once the Americans retook Guam, and we'd gone to live in the orphanage, we'd gotten away from it for a while. But I hadn't forgotten. And on top of everything happening all around me right at that moment, I worried that Benny might be slipping away.

"You think Rita Hayworth will still marry me

when I get back home and propose?" Benny asked. That was Benny. Even in the middle of a horrible disaster he was going to keep things light.

"She's crazy if she doesn't," I answered.

"You're a horrible liar, Patrick O'Donnell. Don't ever get good at it, kid," he said. "C'mon, we gotta try and find out what's goin' on."

Benny hollered and shouted at the crew as we worked our way through them. A couple of sailors asked Teddy and me if we needed help.

"We need help gettin' off this ship, is what we need," Benny said. "Where's them life jackets and rafts?"

But no one ever answered. They didn't seem to know what to do. I overheard one sailor tell another that the first torpedo destroyed the ship's electrical system. His shipmate answered that without it there was no way for instructions to get out to the crew over the ship's loudspeakers.

Benny herded us through the crowd. We kept asking questions and demanding answers, but each response conflicted with the last. The distress call had gone through. It hadn't gone through. The captain had given the order to abandon ship. The captain had given no such order. He was dead. He was alive and on the bridge taking control of the situation right now. No one seemed to know the truth.

The group at the stern was growing in size. Despite orders to the contrary from the few officers there, men continued to ignore them, taking their destiny into their own hands and leaping off the ship. But they didn't realize that even though one of the massive engines had finally died, the other was still running. With one of the *Indianapolis*'s giant propellers still turning, some of those who jumped were bludgeoned to death or chopped into pieces. It was worse than anything I'd seen on Guam. And like I said, I'd seen plenty.

"Don't look, boys! Don't look! Come with me!" Benny said. With his burned arms, he motioned us away from the stern, and we fought our way through the mass of bodies to the port side and back toward the middle of the ship. It was less crowded there, but closer to the fire and smoke, so we huddled down low.

"Patrick," Benny said. "Listen to me. I ain't never lied to you, have I? Not since the day I first met you at Sister Mary Teresa's orphanage and you ticked me off, yakkin' away about how the big bum Hank Greenberg was a better first baseman than the old Iron Horse himself, Lou Gehrig, which even a rock head knows ain't true."

"No, Benny," I said. I was so frightened my breath was coming in ragged gasps. "You've never lied to me."

"Well I ain't lying to you now. I gotta believe the distress call went out. I know I crack on the swabbies a lot, but the *Indianapolis* is a darn good ship. One of the best in the whole fleet. And Captain McVay has everybody trained to do their job. I gotta believe they knew what to do when that stinkin' sub hit us. And the first thing to do would be to send out a call for help. I'm thinkin' there's ships and planes on the way. But I'll tell you true, it don't look good. I don't think this ship is gonna make it. We gotta go over the side. We need to abandon ship. There's guys down there right now in life rafts and they'll pick us up, you'll see.

But we gotta get off the *Indianapolis* before she takes us down with her. You understand me?"

Teddy was clutching my arm again, making his ever-present noise. Teddy understood everything he heard. He knew what was happening all the time. He just never talked. Now he was afraid and clawing at me so much, I couldn't think straight.

"Quiet down, Teddy," I said in the calmest voice I could muster. I needed to focus. But there was no time. I could feel the ship shaking and vibrating beneath my feet. It felt like it was going to break apart at any minute. I knew Benny was right.

I looked out across the dark, tossing waves. It was so hard to see. The sky was overcast. Almost pitch-black and too dark to see anyone floating in the water. Only the fire on board gave off any light at all. But I knew Benny was right. We didn't have a choice. If we stayed on board, we'd die.

"All right, Benny," I said. "I'm ready when you are."

CHAPTER FIVE

INTO THE KILLING SEAS

★ ★ ★

We took one last look around the deck to see if we could find a life jacket. At least one for Teddy. But every one we could spot was already claimed, and the men wearing them didn't look like they'd be giving them up for anyone. The hole the torpedo had cut in the ship had widened with every snap of steel, and now the *Indy* was almost severed in half. Someone was shouting that one of the lifeboats had jammed on its winch. I didn't really know what that meant, only what it meant for us. We were probably going in the water whether I liked it or not.

"I'm not a good swimmer, Benny," I said, starting to lose my nerve. "I'm scared." I wasn't ready for this after all. It was a bad idea.

"It's all right, pipsqueak," Benny said. "We ain't gotta swim nowhere, all we got to do is tread water until help arrives. You can do that. Right, buddy?"

But I was beginning to think I couldn't do it. Back in Guam, when I'd heard that the *Indianapolis* was leaving for the Philippines, all I could think of was getting back there, to find my parents. Now I was on a ship that was going down like the *Titanic* and I was terrified. Why had so much awful stuff happened? We were really the most unlucky kids on God's green earth. Wasn't it bad enough what Teddy and I had been through already?

"I can't do it, Benny," I said. "I'm not gonna be able to swim."

"Sure you can, sport. I promise you someone is out there right now in a raft or one of them flotation nets. Once we give a shout, they'll come right to us. I promise you, champ."

For the first time since I'd met him, I doubted Benny. If the guy selling me on this crazy plan had been Benny at his best—Benjamin Franklin Poindexter, Private First Class United States Marine Corps—I

51

would have been fine. But he was burned and wounded. He couldn't help us much if we got into trouble down there.

"No, Benny, I can't do it," I said.

"It's all right, ace," he said, trying to stand up straight. "I understand. We'll wait until we get . . ."

Benny stopped midsentence, and I looked at him to see what was wrong. He was staring at a wooden pallet, leaning against one of the gun emplacements on the deck. It was about six feet long and four feet wide. I followed Benny over to it and looped my arm through the pallet when he ordered me to pick it up.

"What are we doing, Benny?" I asked. But he didn't answer. He had a weird look in his eyes. Teddy glanced at him, and then back at me, his hand shooting out to grab my free one. I was getting pretty sick of taking Benny's orders without explanation. Maybe this is what it really felt like to be a marine. Benny was pacing now, and he looked pretty agitated. I turned me and Teddy around. I just needed a moment to think. As scared as I was of the water, Benny was scaring me more. He looked determined and confused all at the same time. But before I could figure out why, the ship jerked on its side again. Something smacked me in the back.

"Benny? What are you do—"

I screamed as I flew over the side of the ship.

"Teddy!" I shouted. The word was barely out of my mouth before I saw that my not-so-little brother and that big wooden pallet were following right behind me. The ship was listing so badly, it wasn't as long a drop as it normally would have been. I hit the surface with the worst belly-smacker I'd ever felt in my life. All the air rushed out of my lungs. I plunged below the water's surface hoping to avoid Teddy and the pallet, but I sucked in a great mouthful of water. I heard a loud splash above me and something whacked me hard on the shoulder.

Then somehow I rose to the surface and coughed up all that seawater.

"Heads up, pipsqueak!" I heard Benny shout. "Duck!"

I looked up to see Benny flying through the air. He was going to land right on top of me! Without thinking I dove under once again.

When I bobbed to the surface, Benny and Teddy were there in the water right beside me, the waves raising and lowering us like corks. The pallet floated next to Benny, who'd hooked his arm through it.

"This here pallet is gonna be our raft, boys," Benny said. "No matter what, we ain't gonna let go of it! Understand? You hang on to it like you've never hung on to anything in your life."

"You pushed me into the water!" I screamed at him.

"I didn't. You fell when the ship keeled over. Now hold on to the raft, Patty boy," Benny said calmly.

"No! I'm not doing anything you say anymore!" The waves were running high and when another one crashed into me, I swallowed more water. It hit my stomach and came right back up. As I coughed and retched, Benny paddled over to me, and the next thing I knew, my arms were resting on the pallet, holding my head above water.

"Patrick, calm down now. I'm sorry for what happened to you up there. But you had to get off that ship."

Teddy was clinging to the pallet like a squirrel on an oak tree. His eyes were wild and he was sobbing.

The waves were driving us back toward the side of the ship.

"You pushed me!"

"You already said that, sport. And I get you're mad. You want to believe that, fine. But we got a whole lot worse things to worry about right now."

Almost on cue, I heard a snapping sound and another big piece of the ship broke in the center, snapped off and plunged beneath the surface. The men who were gathered at the stern howled even louder than before. Now they were jumping into the water by the dozens. The ship listed again and twisted farther toward us.

"Patty boy, Teddy, you gotta paddle now! Now! We gotta get away from this ship or it will drag us down with it! Come on now, don't let go of this pallet, and kick those legs as hard as you can!"

I was frightened. Not too frightened to remember I was mad at Benny for pushing me in the ocean. But enough that I knew I had to listen to him now. And I didn't want the ship to fall on us or for us to get sucked under the water. So I kicked with all my might and the pallet slowly moved away from the sinking cruiser.

"Harder, boys!" Benny shouted. "We gotta get farther away!"

Every part of my body hurt and I was exhausted. But my legs kept moving. Even Teddy seemed to understand, grasping the pallet like it was a paddleboard and kicking away like a racehorse.

But the ship was snaking over on its side. The waves were high and heavy, and they kept pushing us back. We weren't going to make it.

"Come on, fellas!" Benny pleaded. "I always heard you Dee-troit boys was tough! This ain't tough. You're swimming like a bunch of pansies. You kick those legs like United States Marines! Go! Go!"

He was pushing us. Hard. It just made me even angrier at him. But I guess that's what I needed in that moment. Anger forcing me to prove to Benny that I *wasn't* a pansy. That I was tough. I furiously kicked my legs, and we gained distance from the ship. The pallet was unwieldy and hard to maneuver, but slowly we cut through the waves.

"That's it!" Benny prodded us. "Now we're doing it."

As we were about to crest another wave, the loud wrenching sound of metal behind us told me the ship had finally rolled onto its side. It made a huge splash and before I could do anything, the suction of the ship sinking below the water jerked me away from the pallet. I tried to take a breath before I went under, but all I got was a mouthful of salt water.

The last thing I heard was Benny shouting my name.

CHAPTER SIX

ONE LAST THING

★ ★ ★

Down I went.

I was wrapped in an air bubble, but I didn't dare try to breathe. On Guam I'd heard sailors talk about this very thing happening. When a ship sunk, it created suction all around it and pulled down anything that was near. I used to go by the port and listen to the sailors tell stories to each other. One day a guy had been talking about being aboard the USS *Hammann*, which was sunk in the Battle of Midway.

"Got caught in an air bubble," he said. "That old tub wanted to pull me right down to Davy Jones's locker with her. But I said 'No thank you, Captain Jones,' and managed to kick my way back up. Almost didn't make it . . ."

I realized that was what was happening to me. Pieces of debris from the ship—chunks of wood and broken railings—were rising up from below like rockets shooting into the sky and crashing into me. Murky, dark masses clouded the water. Leaking diesel fuel, I guessed. But strangely enough, I could see something past it: the fire still raging through the portholes of the ship. There must have been some air left in the dogged-off sections of the interior. The flames continued as the giant iron beast sank slowly toward the ocean floor. Other than the soft glow of the firelight, the ocean was black as night.

I tried mightily to pull myself upward, but the suction was far too strong. I felt helpless and tired. I pumped my legs until I had no strength left. I kicked and kicked. It was no good. My legs were exhausted and I sank even deeper into the dark water.

I'm not sure when the realization came to me. I was going to die. *What does somebody do when they're going to die and they know it?* From the first night the Japanese attacked Guam, and for the next two years, I'd seen or knew someone who died nearly every day. But I never really wondered what they thought about when it was happening to them. Some of them cried, some shrieked. Some of them accepted their death quietly. Some, like Sister Felicity, never knew what hit them. It was just the end and that was all. I guess I'd just put it out of my mind, never figuring what I'd do when my time came.

I didn't know what to do. Should I pray? If Sister Mary Teresa were there she'd say I should ask God for forgiveness of my sins. Should I apologize to my mother because I hadn't done what I'd promised? I hadn't taken care of Teddy like she asked me to. What would happen to Teddy? Would he drown in the heaving ocean, as I was about to do?

I thought about a million things in those few seconds. My lungs were about to burst. I couldn't hold my breath any longer. My eyes were burning from the salt water and I wanted to cry, but I was afraid to even do that. I would hold on to my last breath. Someday, when we met in heaven, my mother would know I tried. To my last breath, I tried.

Then I heard it. The faint sound of a familiar voice calling my name.

Something came over me. That voice was calling me home. It pleaded with me, and I couldn't resist answering. I started pushing and kicking against the water with energy that I'd have sworn I didn't have. At last the air bubble separated from the relentless downward pull of the ship, and I darted toward the surface.

Below me, the last flickering flames of the ship were fading to black. Faster and faster I sped upward until I burst out of the water and shot several feet into the air before I splashed back down again. Like those broken pieces of the ship that had bombarded me only moments earlier, the sea had swallowed me, and now it was spitting me back out. I sucked in a great, heaving lungful of air before a wave crashed into me, knocking me under again. But nothing was pulling me down now, and I kicked my way back to the surface.

It was still dark and I couldn't see anything. I furiously treaded water. And then I heard that familiar voice again.

"Patty boy! Patrick O'Donnell of Dee-troit, Michigan, you call out! Sound off right now!" Benny bellowed. His voice was hoarse and raw, like he'd just swallowed broken glass. But he was shouting as loudly as he could.

"I'm here, Benny!"

"Patty boy?"

"I'm h—" Another wave crashed into me, knocking the words from my mouth; I tumbled over in the water again. I decided right then that I really hated the ocean. Really hated it a lot.

I emerged again and tried to get into a rhythm with the rising and falling waves so I didn't get swamped every second. Benny was still yelling my name.

"Patrick!"

"I'm here! Benny, I'm here!"

"Where are you, pipsqueak?"

"In the ocean somewhere? It's pitch-black! How am I supposed to know where I am?" I was still a little shook up from almost drowning. I probably shouldn't have taken it out on Benny. But still.

"Patty boy! You gotta try to swim to my voice! Come on, now! You can do it!"

"I can't, Benny! Too tired. I almost drowned. I can't—"

Like always, Benny refused to give up.

"You listen to me, you will *not* drown in this ocean. Benjamin Franklin Poindexter, Private First Class, United States Marine Corps will not allow it. Is that clear to you, marine? You will promise me right now at this very moment that you are not gonna drown. You are gonna survive. Is that clear? Sound off!"

Benny had turned into his old self. Well, maybe his old self, if he'd ever become a drill instructor. When I didn't answer right away he started cursing again and calling my name. I kept trying to tread water, but I was so tired. If only I'd gotten my hands on one of those life jackets . . .

"Patrick!" Benny croaked again. The more he yelled, the worse his voice got.

"Benny, I can't swim anymore!" I said, bobbing on another wave.

"You can't swim anymore? Well, cry me a flippin' river, sport! You think you got problems? I'm stuck on a lousy hunk of wood with your screamin' brother. I dang near got my face burnt off! So don't you sing me none of your sob stories about how bad you got it.

There's about a thousand men in this ocean right now got it just as bad off as you! Or worse. And that ain't countin' the ones that's already dead. So you quit your bellyachin' and you swim toward the sound of my voice! You do it now! You hear me, marine?"

Before I even realized what I was doing, I was dog-paddling toward his voice.

"I don't know how to swim, Benny! I'm afraid!"

"You don't know how to swim? You think I had a pool in the backyard of my third floor walk-up in the Bronx? You kick with your legs and paddle with your hands. It ain't algebra. Now, my hands and face ain't worth a plug nickel, but my legs is workin' and me and Teddy is gonna kick our legs and push this pallet toward you. You keep hollerin' and I'll do the same. Follow my voice. Then we'll meet in the middle!"

I didn't answer because I was concentrating hard on not being dunked beneath the waves and trying to figure out where Benny was in the swirling blackness of the dark sea.

"Patty boy! You hear me!"

"Yeah, Benny, I'm here!"

"I can't see nothin'. You gotta keep shoutin' so I know which way to swim, you rock head!"

"I don't . . . I can't . . ." I was out of breath and dipping underwater again. If something didn't happen soon, I wasn't going to make it.

"The starting lineup for the 1940 Dee-troit Tigers! You shout it out to me! That's an order, marine!"

I was spent. My arms stopped moving. Each one felt like it weighed a million pounds. A part of me wanted to just slip beneath the water. But then I heard Teddy. Benny was somewhere close by, because Teddy's ever-present wailing carried over the water.

"Come on, Patty Boy! You think them Motor City Kitties is so much better than the Bronx Bombers, give me that lineup! Who played catcher?"

"Birdie Tebbetts!" I shouted back.

"First base!"

"Rudy York!"

Benny shouted, "Yeah, Rudy York! Couldn't field a ground ball with a shovel and he was still better than that bum Greenberg. Who couldn't carry the Iron Horse's jockstrap, by the way!"

"In your dreams!" I shouted back. I started paddling again.

"Second base!"

"Charlie Gehringer!"

"Third base!"

I tried to remember. My brain wasn't working right.

"Bartell! Dickie Bartell," I hollered.

"Shortstop!"

"Pinky Higgins!"

"Right field!" Benny sounded closer, and Teddy's wailing was growing louder, out there in the darkness.

"Petey Fox, then Bruce Campbell after the trade," I shouted back.

"Center field!" Benny shouted. He was close now, and as I rose on a wave I thought I could see the dim outline of two figures in the water, moving toward me.

"Barney McCosky!" I yelled.

"Left field!"

"Hank Greenberg! And he won the MVP after moving to left field from first base so the team could trade for Rudy York. Did the Iron Horse ever win MVP at two different positions, Benny?"

"I still say he's a bum!" Benny's hoarse voice called back. "Who's gonna be your starting pitcher if you gotta win one game, pipsqueak! Come on now, we're close! I can tell. Don't you dare give up!"

I was nearly out of breath and my legs were cramping badly. But Benny's voice sounded closer, and Teddy's cries were nearly drowning him out. *Just a little longer*, I thought to myself.

"Patty, who's your starting pitcher?"

"Bobo . . . Newsom." I was panting and could hardly speak anymore. "No! Wait! Bobo had a better record that year, but I'd give the ball to Schoolboy Rowe. The pressure wouldn't—"

I never got to finish. A wave rose up and the pallet crashed into me, nearly knocking me under again. And there were Benny and Teddy. Teddy even stopped crying when he realized it was me. All I could see in the darkness was the whites of their eyes. I grabbed the pallet and managed to pull myself up onto it, so only my legs hung in the water.

"You'd make a lousy manager, pipsqueak," Benny said. "Pickin' Schoolboy over Bobo. Madness. Everybody knows you gotta ride the hot-hand."

CHAPTER SEVEN

THE DARKEST DEPTHS

★ ★ ★

30 JULY 1945, DAY ONE

I'm not sure how long I lay asleep half in and half out of the water. It could have been hours or minutes. When I came to, I was still clinging to the pallet and Teddy was whimpering softly, something he often did in his fitful sleep. The night sky was still dark, but it was growing lighter far off on the horizon. When the moon cracked its way through the clouds, I could see Benny floating along, his burned hands twisted in between the wooden slats of our makeshift life raft. He groaned and muttered soft curses under his breath.

The sea had calmed some, and the waves were not quite as high as they'd been before. Still, even the smaller ones tossed us about. I wished I could find a way to get some height and have a look around, but I was still so exhausted, my head and shoulders remained planted on the wood.

As I wiped the sleep from my eyes, I realized that we weren't as alone at sea as I'd thought. Everywhere around us, voices were all yelling at once. From the sound of it, a whole bunch of the crew had managed to abandon ship. But from their cries for help it was also clear a great many of them were injured.

"Where's the doc? I got a wounded man here!" I heard a husky voice call.

The doctor!

Every ship had at least one doctor plus several medical corpsmen. If I could find one of them, maybe they could help Benny. As if he knew I was thinking about him, he moaned, lifted his head, and looked around.

"Patrick? You still there, pipsqueak?"

"I'm right here, Benny," I said.

"Good. We bein' rescued yet?"

"Nah, not yet. The sun will be up soon and I hear a lot of guys yelling for help, but I don't see them. Or any help for us," I said.

"Yeah. With these waves, I'll bet our guys is scattered everywhere. Hard keepin' track in the dark—" Benny stopped talking and groaned. It sounded like he was in agony.

"What's wrong, Benny?" I asked.

"Nothing, sport. Just a rough start to the mornin' is all. I don't suspect this salt water is doing these burns I got any good."

I didn't know what to say. If we were in the jungle, I could have found lots of things to help Benny. Fresh water, plants that would help his burns heal, even mud packed on the wounds would stop infection and ease the pain. The Chamorro taught me a lot about survival and living off the land.

In the jungle. Not the middle of the ocean.

But maybe one of Benny's shipmates could help him. Their voices sounded like they were coming from all directions.

"Where's the doctor?" the husky voice shouted again.

"I think that's Colosi," Benny whispered. He'd mentioned the marine from Chicago before. "Voice sounds like fingernails on a chalkboard."

"No one's seen him," another sailor answered back. "But I know he made it off the ship! Doc! Doc! You out there?"

I heard someone else answer, but they were too far away to understand.

"That's him! That's Doc!" Colosi said. "We gotta swim toward him, I got a wounded man here!"

"Help! Over here!" I shouted.

"Who goes there?" a voice came back.

"We're hurt. There's an injured marine here!" I said.

No one answered.

"Listen up, pipsqueak," Benny rasped. "I know Colosi. I don't like him. He's trouble. I think you oughta stay away from him and his bunch until sunup. Find somebody else out there, *capisce*?"

Benny groaned, and though it was dark and nearly impossible to see, I had the sense that he had passed out again. At any rate, he was silent. I thought about what he said. He didn't like that Sergeant Stenkevitz back on the ship. And Stenkevitz seemed like a jerk. Now he was telling me to stay away from this guy Colosi. Maybe I should listen to him. What if Colosi and his friends tried to take the pallet away from us? What would we do then?

More men shouted out to each other from somewhere. The noise and size of the waves made it difficult to determine where their voices were coming from. It still wasn't light enough yet to see much. But I had an idea.

"Benny?"

He groaned incoherently.

"Benny!" I shouted.

"What!" he said. I could tell I startled him awake.

"Can you swim? Paddle, I mean? Help me push the pallet through the water?"

"I don't know, buddy," he said. "I'm plumb wore out. If I could rest awhile, I might be able to help. Why?"

"Because I just heard more of the crew shouting over there about the doctor. He got off the ship with the rest of the survivors. If we can find him, maybe he can treat your burns."

"That's a real good idea, pipsqueak. You're thinkin' like a marine. Makin' an assessment of your tactical situation. Choosin' your course of action. But here's the thing. Your troops is done in, Patty boy. Teddy is too wrung out to help. And as much as it pains Benjamin Franklin Poindexter, Private First Class, United States Marine Corps to say it, I ain't fit for duty right now. Besides, I'll bet that doc's waitin' room is full up right now. Lotta wounded he's gotta tend to. Assumin' it was even him them swabbies heard. We should just wait here. Someone will be along to rescue us soon," he said.

Something was different in Benny. Never once could I remember him saying not to do a thing, or that we weren't going to find a way to accomplish what we set out to do. Benny was always upbeat and positive. Except for swabbies, Tojo, Hirohito, Hank Greenberg, and Sergeant Stenkevitz, he never had anything bad to say about anything. Now he was making up a reason, an excuse not to try something. I figured it was my turn to get him going.

"You always told me marines never give up," I said.

"Hey now! Whoa. Whoa. Whoa." Benny was almost whispering, his voice was so weak. "Don't you go spoutin' off about quittin'. I ain't sayin' that. We ain't givin' up. Not one bit. But even a squared-away marine has gotta rest and regroup before the next fight. Best thing we can do is hunker down and wait till daylight. By then the rescue ships and planes will be here and we'll get plucked right out of this giant bathtub like a rubber duck. I think we just need to rest until then, all right, Patty boy?"

"I guess," I said. But I wasn't convinced Benny was right. I was thinking about the chaos on board the ship when the torpedoes hit. How fast the *Indianapolis* went down. I remembered some of the crew saying nobody knew for sure if the distress call went out. How the communication system got all blown up with the first hit. Nobody even knew when to abandon ship, because the speakers didn't work. I wasn't sure Benny was thinking clearly. Maybe nobody was coming for us. At least not for a while.

I rested for a few minutes. The pallet was doing an admirable job of keeping me afloat. I had no idea which direction was which, but there was light starting to break off the horizon to my left, so I knew that must be east. I heard some guys shouting again. Not Colosi—some voices I didn't recognize, coming from behind me. I was reminded again about the doctor.

If Benny and Teddy couldn't help, it didn't matter. I could. I worked around to Teddy's side of the pallet and started kicking with my legs, pushing it slowly toward the sound of the voices. I wasn't making much progress. But it was something.

After a while, I was getting closer. The voices were getting louder, clearer. And suddenly I could make out what the men were shouting. Dozens of them. They weren't calling for the doctor anymore. They were screaming for their lives.

"No! Dear God! No!" I heard a single voice cry out. "Help! Someone please help me!" More voices joined in. I heard a high-pitched, almost squeaky voice from somebody who sounded young and terrified. A gruff, hoarse cry—probably someone from New York, because he sounded like Benny—only with a deeper tone. Then a southern accent shouted out in horror, joining an overwhelming chorus of screams. They sounded as if they were being tortured. Then the younger-sounding voice spelled out the reason for their alarm, and I instantly grew terrified myself.

"Sharks!" he yelled. "Everywhere! Look out—"
His words died in his throat, and he made the most horrifying, anguished sound I'd ever heard. On Guam, when someone was shot, death usually came quickly. A bullet ripped into someone's chest, and that was it for them. Or sometimes in the jungle we had to leave our wounded behind, because when you're being hunted by the Japanese Imperial Army, silence is life and noise is death. And the wounded tend to make noise. I tried not to think about the ones we'd abandoned. The Japanese always caught up with them quickly. Usually you'd hear a single gunshot. And then their cries would stop.

Now it was sharks. There were sharks in the water. And from the sound of it, they were all around those men. I stopped paddling and floated there, waiting for someone, *anyone*, to tell me what to do. Benny was too far gone at the moment to realize what was happening.

And then, below the surface of the water, something hard and scaly brushed against my leg.

The sharks had found us.

And just like the other men had, I screamed.

CHAPTER EIGHT

RELENTLESS

★ ★ ★

A hh! Ahh!" I shrieked again, sounding a lot like Teddy. I climbed up on the pallet, trying desperately to get my entire body out of the water and onto the wooden surface. Clambering up and onto it, I landed right next to Benny, who came awake with a shout.

"Whoa! Patty boy, what are you doing? What's wrong?"

I was too scared to speak. The pallet was tipping and Benny was sliding off.

"Hang on, sport! Calm down now, little buddy. You're gonna tip us over."

Benny looked me in the eye and tried to calm me down.

"Patrick, listen to me now. You're gonna tip us over. This hunk of wood is going to take us all down with it, if you don't settle down. You're scared. I understand. But look over there." He pointed with one of his clawed stumps. The eastern horizon was reddening now.

"The sun is rising. That means help is coming, pipsqueak. So calm yourself and tell Benny what—"

A piercing, ear-shattering scream carried across the water and cut him off.

"NO! Please! Oh God noooo!" It was the southerner. But he wasn't the only one in danger.

"Look out! Stay together! Back-to-back!" he yelled.

Benny looked at me with his eyes wide.

"What's going on? Tell me, Patty, tell me what's happening. Has the sub come back? Sometimes those stinkin' subs will resurface after they sunk a tub and machine-gun any survivors in the water. You hear anything that sounded like gunfire?"

I shook my head.

Benny got right in my face.

"Patrick," he said calmly. "You gotta tell me

what's going on. Benny can't help if I don't know what's happenin'."

"They ... they said there ... were ... sharks! I heard men scream and ..."

"And what? And what, Patty boy?"

"I was in the water. Trying to ... to push ... the pallet, and something bumped against me. Brushed my leg and ... and it was hard and scaly. And I screamed and climbed up here."

Benny looked around at the water. The waves were calming down as the sun rose, and it was easier to see. Far off in the distance I could finally see some of the men I'd heard in the darkness. Most of them were wearing life jackets, and they had fastened them together somehow. They looked like a map I'd seen of the Philippines, dozens of individual islands bobbing on the water. But these islands moved, twitching and jerking and pointing in every direction.

"You saw a shark?" Benny asked, looking back at me.

"No ... no ... I felt it bump up against my leg," I said.

"All right," Benny said. "You did the right thing. Climbin' up here like you did. But I gotta tell you, it probably weren't a shark. These swabbies, they're hurt, they been out in the water all night. They're tired and waterlogged. And what happens is your mind starts playing tricks and you hallucinate, see . . ."

"Oh, God, it's Ballard!" Benny was interrupted right at that moment by the southern man's voice ringing out. We both looked and saw what he was shouting about. The dead body of a crewman bobbed in the water halfway between the floating crew and our pallet. And circling around the body, I spotted several large fins.

"Don't look, Patty," Benny said. "Don't look." I saw him glance over at Teddy, who tossed restlessly in his sleep. Benny had been telling me not to look at bad things ever since the ship went down. But I couldn't draw my eyes away from the slowly circling fins.

There were three of them, dark triangles cutting through the water like the prow of a ship. The crewman floated facedown in the water, making no effort to swim away from the danger that was bearing down on him and drawing nearer every second. He was obviously dead.

It happened fast.

One of the fins darted away from the others and lunged toward the body. The water splashed and churned and then just like that, the dead man disappeared below the ocean surface. He was gone. The other two sharks followed, and the water soon calmed again.

"You did the right thing, pipsqueak," Benny said. "Don't you think you didn't. Heck, if one of them critters bumped up against me, I'd a done a lot more than yell. But you listen to me now. Help is on the way. There's two things your United States Navy is good at. One is giving us marines a ride when we gotta go do the fightin' somewhere. The second is pickin' up their crews when one of these rust buckets unexpectedly loses its ability to float. It's going to be all right, you'll see. Or my name ain't Benjamin Franklin—"

"Poindexter, Private First Class of the United States Marines," I finished for him.

"You see?" Benny chuckled. His laugh was coarse and rough like someone had scrubbed the inside of his throat with sandpaper. "Now you're beginning to think like a jarhead. Like a straight-up, squared-away marine."

The pallet was still tipping. It felt like I was going to fall back into the ocean, which was the last place I wanted to be. I scrabbled backward on my butt, away from the edge. The pallet tilted more and we all nearly fell in.

"Whoa!" Benny croaked. "We gotta spread out, pipsqueak." He struggled to move himself over the rough surface of the wood but finally made it into a corner. We were now like three points on a triangle drawn inside a square. The pallet righted itself, and I felt a little better. I made sure no part of my body was touching the water.

"There we go," Benny rasped. "We should be fine now. All we gotta do is sit back until the SAR teams come looking for us."

"What does SAR mean, Benny?"

"It means 'search and rescue.' The navy'll send out

ships and planes looking for us. Probably planes first. Then they'll radio our coordinates and send a ship to pick us up."

We floated there a minute. Benny lay his head back down and drifted off to sleep. The sun finally cleared the horizon and I felt the heat rise instantly. It was still humid, but I started thinking maybe Benny was right. We might be okay. If our luck held, we'd get rescued sometime that day. But of course, we weren't very lucky.

Thirty yards away, a large black fin popped out of the water.

One of the sharks was back, and it started swimming directly toward us.

"Benny!" I couldn't help it. I shouted as loud as I could. The fin kept coming, heading straight for our raft. It looked impossibly big in the water. It was twenty yards away, then ten.

"Benny!"

He finally lifted his head up, but he was groggy.

"Wha . . ." he mumbled. I knew he had to be in horrible pain, but I didn't know what else to do.

"Look!" I said, pointing at the approaching shark.

Benny struggled to sit up. He had trouble focusing his eyes, but when he saw the giant fish, he sat up straighter.

"Holy—" Benny never got to finish what was probably another curse. Because the shark dived beneath us, lifted the pallet into the air, and tilted it to the side. We nearly tumbled into the water. Teddy awoke with a start and immediately started whimpering.

"Teddy! Quiet!" I said. He stopped making his noise. Somehow, during the worst times in the jungle on Guam, I'd taught Teddy to listen to me. To be quiet when the Japanese patrols went by. He'd do it. But it was real hard for him. I don't know how he learned it, whether it was the tone of my voice or a certain look on my face. Whatever it was, he knew when I meant business, and he'd calm down.

The pallet rocked as the shark thrashed beneath it.

"Hold on, boys! Hold on, now!" Benny shouted.

But I didn't want to hold on. The spaces in between the slats of the pallet were exposed to the water and I envisioned the shark pushing through them to bite off my hands. But it didn't. As quickly as it had come, it disappeared into the ocean and our makeshift raft stopped shaking.

We all sat there a moment in stunned silence. Finally I mustered up the courage to speak.

"What . . . what was that thing doing?" I said. Teddy rocked back and forth to soothe himself.

"Lookin' for its next meal. I expect it's gone now," he said. "I've heard plenty of stories about sharks. Don't know what's true and what ain't. But one thing I heard is they're eatin' machines. They basically swim and eat. So if he's swum away, it means he ain't found nothin' to suit his fancy here. Shoot, I ain't nothin' but bone and muscle and you two together is barely an appetizer. Ain't no shark gonna come back and eat us."

"I don't know, Benny," I said. "That was awful close. What about before? That body . . ." I stopped because I didn't want to think about what happened to the dead man we'd seen earlier. Ballard. I know he was already dead, but still.

"That was different. That was an easy target for the shark. If he comes back here again, he knows

Benny Poindexter is going to give him a pop on the kisser that would make the Brown Bomber proud. And then he's gonna get a quick lesson in what's what, *capisce?*"

Benny was weak and basically helpless. With his curled-up, burned hands, he couldn't punch a pillow, much less a shark. But the look on Benny's face was what struck me the most. For the first time since I'd known him, I saw Benjamin Franklin Poindexter, Private First Class, United States Marine Corps, born in the Bronx in New York, fan of the hated Yankees and lover of Lindy's cheesecake, with a look on his face I'd never seen before.

And that look was fear.

CHAPTER NINE

NUMBERS

★ ★ ★

Teddy drifted into one of his agitated sleeps. He was never at peace, and it seemed like he was always exhausted. At the orphanage he would fall asleep sometimes during school, but Sister Mary Teresa usually just let him rest. Every so often she would walk over to his desk, where he sat with his head resting on his folded arms. He was plagued by bad dreams, and if he whimpered or moaned, she reached out to pat his head or rub the back of his neck. It wasn't like Teddy couldn't do things. He ate his food and took baths and dressed himself and all the things a normal person does. When we lived with the Chamorro in the jungle he would do what I told him most of the time. But he scared so easily and he was upset all the time. It was a wonder we were never captured. And he would not speak. Not ever. No matter how I tried. Whatever was going on in his head had to wear him out, so he slept all the time. Maybe it was just his way of escaping from all the bad things we'd seen. Now I felt guilty for bringing him on the ship. He would have been safer with Sister Mary Teresa. Why had I done it?

Once he was asleep, I scooted back across the pallet so it rebalanced. The sun was low in the sky, but well above the horizon now. It was growing hotter by the second. I scanned the water but didn't see any sign of sharks. I sat cross-legged, not wanting to lie down like Benny and Teddy in case the sharks came back.

"Patty boy," Benny croaked. "I think you better get yourself a drink of fresh water."

"That'd be great," I said. "I sure wish we had some."

"Patty?"

"Yes, Benny?"

"Look at your belt," he said.

I looked down to see the canteen I had clipped to my belt when the ship exploded. In all the chaos I completely forgot about it. It was a one-quart metal canteen with a screw-on cap. Throughout all the excitement, it had stayed attached to my belt.

"Huh," I said.

"They raise 'em bright in Dee-troit," Benny cracked.

I took the canteen off my belt and shook it.

"Uh-oh," I said.

"What?" Benny asked.

"It's only about half full," I said. "When I heard the explosion, I grabbed it. I don't know why. But I probably grabbed the one Teddy and I were drinking out of."

"Patrick?" Benny said.

"Yes?"

"You see any drinkin' fountains or other canteens of water floating around? Maybe a drugstore we could pop into and get a soda pop?"

I couldn't help it. Benny made me laugh.

"Nope. I guess a little water is better than none. Right?"

I took a swig. The water tasted like heaven on my

tongue. I wanted to drain the canteen, but Benny gave me a warning.

"Gotta save some, chief," he said. "Teddy will be needing a drink when he wakes up. And we might all need to share it." I held it out to him, but he waved it away.

"My mouth don't feel right, sport," he said. "You keep it for now. Save some for me. I'll drink it later."

"I thought you said the SAP teams would be here soon?" I said.

Benny laughed. "SAR teams. Search and rescue. But I don't know when they'll be here for sure. One thing I do know about swabbies is none of them is ever on time. Your marines is punctual. The navy likes to take things slowly. So let's be smart and preserve our supplies until we get more of an idea. Sound good?"

I put the cap back on the canteen, fastening it to my belt. But I was thinking about what Benny said, about rescuers coming to save us. And I was wondering if maybe he wasn't telling me the whole truth. I knew sometimes adults thought that because you were a kid you shouldn't know or see things. As far as I knew,

Benny had never lied to me before. But I heard doubt in his voice when he talked about us getting rescued. Maybe he wasn't being untruthful on purpose— maybe he just didn't know.

As the morning passed and the heat rose, the sharks left us for deeper waters. The ocean surface was mostly smooth now, with just a small rolling chop to the waves. Shading my eyes, I gazed across the water looking for the large group of floating crewmen. They were farther away than they had been at dawn, the currents sending us drifting apart. I'd been thinking that maybe we could paddle their way and join up with them. Maybe they'd found the doctor. He could help Benny.

In between us and them was the smaller band of men we'd heard talking earlier in the darkness. There were six of them, and they looked pretty miserable. Most of the men had cuts and burns on their faces. A couple of them bobbed along with their heads down. They looked exhausted and scared.

"That one in the front of the group—the little squirt, face all pinched up like a weasel—that's Colosi," Benny said. "He's trouble."

I said nothing as I watched them. For now they didn't seem to notice us, or if they did they weren't paying us much attention. Until suddenly they were. I saw one of them point us out to his buddies as the distance between us lessened.

"Patrick," Benny said. "I ain't feeling so good. I'm trying to stay awake, but my hands and face is killing me. I need to close my eyes. You keep an eye on Colosi and that bunch. They get too close you give a holler, *capisce*?" Benny eyes were shut before I even got a chance to answer him.

The sun rose and so did the temperature as the current drew Colosi's group nearer to our raft. When they were close enough I could see they had tied themselves together with the straps on their life jackets. It kept the waves from separating them. Two of them propped up a grievously injured man.

Colosi squinted at me in the bright sun. "Who are you?" he called out.

I didn't answer; I just stared back at him. I'm not sure why. I just felt like if I did, something bad might happen. My skin tingled and my heart beat faster. Time seemed to slow down a little. I remembered feeling the same way in the jungle. Sometimes you just got a sense that the Japanese were coming, and you faded away into the underbrush or took cover. Blood rushed in my ears and my hands got a little shaky.

"Who are you?" he asked again.

"I . . . I'm . . . from the ship. The *Indianapolis*," I said.

"Why ain't you in uniform?" Colosi said.

I didn't answer.

"We got a wounded man here. We need your raft. Where'd you get it?" he pestered me.

I tried to think of what to say. If only Benny would wake up and tell me what to do. He knew how to handle people like Colosi. I didn't.

"I . . . I got . . . I got my own wounded," I stammered.

"What's your name, sailor?" Colosi asked. I looked down at my shaking hands. My arms and clothes were spotted with black diesel fuel. I could feel it caking on my face. It probably made it hard for them to tell I wasn't a regular part of the crew. And Benny and Teddy were curled up on the pallet.

"O'Donnell," I said.

"Where you from, O'Donnell?" he asked.

I remembered Benny telling Sergeant Stenkevitz about all the new crew coming aboard the *Indianapolis* before leaving Guam. And how they were going to do training exercises along the way. There were probably lots of unfamiliar faces. If I kept quiet, maybe they wouldn't know I was just a kid from Detroit.

"Michigan," I said.

"That right? I got a cousin in Michigan," he said. "Listen, you're gonna have to give over that pallet you're floating on. We need to put our wounded man on it."

I shook my head. "I got my own wounded," I said again.

"You refusing us?" Colosi's eyes narrowed. His chin was sharp and pointed, and I couldn't help but think Benny was right. He did look like a weasel.

"No," I said. "Just saying I got injured men, too. I'll take your man on if you want, but we can't give up the pallet. We got no life jackets."

"We'll trade you life jackets for the pallet," he insisted.

"I don't think so," I said.

Even though his face was all cut up and bleeding, I could see Colosi was getting mad.

"You little . . ." Colosi started to say.

"Colosi, leave him alone . . ." one of the other men said.

"Shut up, Dumbrowski," Colosi said. "We need that raft for Keller."

"Colosi . . ." Dumbrowski said. "Keller is already dead."

"No he ain't!" Colosi turned and shouted at the guy named Dumbrowski. "You ain't a doctor. We're taking that raft and we're putting Keller on it and getting him to the doc, you understand?" Colosi stared hard at Dumbrowski, who looked away. The other men in Colosi's group remained silent. He turned his attention back to me.

"Hand over that raft, sailor," he said to me.

"Benny," I said quietly. He didn't respond. I tried to imagine what he'd do in this situation.

"What do you say?" Colosi demanded.

"I said, I can't give you the raft. I got my own injured here. I can take on your wounded man, but that's all I can do. We don't have life jackets. If I give you the raft, we'll drown."

Colosi's eyes darted back and forth as if he were measuring the distance between his group and the pallet. I didn't know what to do. I only knew I would never let him take this tiny hunk of wood away from us.

"We're taking that pallet," Colosi said. He attempted to untie himself from the group of floating men but was having trouble with the knot. No matter how hard he tried he couldn't get it undone. "Come on! Come on!" he shouted. Struggling in the water, he cursed and yanked and finally broke free. He splashed through the water, paddling his way toward us. I raised myself up on my knees.

"Benny!" I whispered. He didn't stir. He had to have been in horrible pain, otherwise there was no way he would have let me face this alone.

I watched, my eyes locked on Colosi as he cut the distance to us in half. Then he was just a few short yards away.

"Get back," I said.

"No," Colosi shot back, breathing hard from his swim.

Something caught my eye. I looked up at Dumbrowski and the others. They were paddling away! The rest of the group, with Keller's lifeless body strapped to them, swam toward the large group of men that now floated far to the west.

"We're taking that raft," Colosi said. He'd paddled close enough that with a few more strokes he could grab the pallet. And if he did, it would be no problem for him to tip it over and dump us off. I looked around for any kind of weapon. My eyes settled on my shoes. I slipped them off.

"I'm warning you, stay away," I said.

Colosi laughed. He was still laughing when my right shoe hit him in the forehead. He squawked in surprise.

"I told you to back off," I said. "We're not giving up our raft."

"Let's get him, boys," he said, unaware he was now operating alone. Colosi lunged at the raft, grabbing hold of it with one hand and pulling it toward him.

It jerked beneath us, causing me to tumble over to my side. Teddy woke up screaming. Benny moaned but didn't regain consciousness. I scrambled back to my knees and pounded on Colosi's hand with my other shoe.

"Ow!" he yelled. He reached up, snatched a fistful of my wet shirt, and tried to pull me into the water. I hooked my feet in the spaces between the boards and hit him as hard as I could with the shoe, this time across the face. But Colosi was stronger than me. He lurched up out of the water, hoisted himself onto the pallet, and grabbed me by the throat. In an instant he slammed me down on the boards. My knees wrenched backward at an unnatural angle, and the air rushed out of my lungs with a whoosh.

"Give . . . it . . . to . . . me . . ." he shouted. His eyes were full of rage. I couldn't breathe. I hammered his head with the shoe, but it had no effect, so I dropped it and smacked his hands with my own. His grip was like iron.

"No!" I wheezed. "Teddy . . . Benny . . . help . . . me . . ." The world was getting dark and my vision was clouding. My hands fell away from Colosi's. One of them bumped against the canteen clipped to my belt. I tugged it loose and with the last remaining strength I had, I smashed it against the side of Colosi's head. Once. Twice. Three times. The third time, I must have hit his temple, because he grunted and fell back into the water.

His face had a new cut, and fresh blood dribbled down his cheek. It made me feel good. I was tired and weak, but I crawled back up on my knees and sucked in great ragged gasps of breath. I hoped Colosi would just go away, but he was still treading water. And still looking like he'd kill me for the pallet.

"I told you," he said. "Me and my boys are taking this raft."

"It looks like your *boys* left you behind," I said.

"What?" Colosi said, giving me a hard stare.

"See?" I said, pointing behind him.

"What are you doing?! Come back!" Colosi screamed. His head swiveled back and forth between me and his friends, who were floating farther away by the minute. Colosi looked scared and confused, unsure why he was being abandoned.

"No wait! Wait!" Finally he made his choice and paddled after his shipmates. I watched as he plunged through the water in pursuit. None of the group looked back at him as he called after them.

I slumped back on my haunches, breathing hard. The canteen was dented and my other shoe was missing. I looked up in time to watch Colosi try in vain to catch his fellow crewmen. He was a good two hundred yards away from them when a dark dorsal fin broke the water's surface behind him.

"Colosi! Look out!" I shouted.

He never heard me.

CHAPTER TEN

THE SECOND NIGHT

★ ★ ★

30 JULY 1945

After the encounter with Colosi, I collapsed into an exhausted sleep. When I awoke it was dark with just a bit of moonlight shining through the clouds. I must have slept the entire day. Careful not to rock the pallet, I sat up. The canteen was lying next to me. Opening it, I took a small sip of water. Teddy was curled into a ball with his hands and arms covering his head.

I poked him on the shoulder.

"Teddy," I said softly. "Teddy, wake up."

He didn't move.

"Teddy?" I poked him a little harder. It startled him and he sat up with a shout.

"Aaah!"

"Easy, Teddy," I said. "It's just me. Now listen to me. I'm going to give you some water. But this is all we have." I held out the canteen and shook it, the water making a splashing sound. "You can just take a couple small sips and try not to spill any of it, okay?"

Teddy looked at me and nodded. Ever since we landed on Guam and Teddy stopped speaking, he'd had a hard time doing some of the smaller normal things a person does. In the orphanage, at dinnertime he would often spill his drink or drop his plate. In the morning he'd have trouble tying his shoes or brushing his teeth. He could do the major stuff, but the little details gave him trouble. Back home, my dad had this Glenn Miller Orchestra record he played all the time. Somehow it got scratched, and when it played one of the songs, it would skip back and forth, making the music sound all jumbled up. I always thought of that record when Teddy acted up. He'd just get stuck on a thing like a shoestring or a button and not be able to work his way past it.

I held out the canteen and Teddy snatched it from my hands. He took a huge gulp of water. I grabbed it back so he wouldn't finish it all, and he wailed so hard that some of it spilled.

"Dang it, Teddy!" I yelled. He started to cry. I screwed the cap back on the canteen and set it on the pallet next to me.

"Hey, sport," Benny muttered. Finally awake, he was lying on his back. If I was being honest, the rest hadn't done him any good. He looked and sounded even worse. "Take it easy on him, Patty boy. He's just scared. I know you been through just as much as he has, but you ain't Teddy. You can handle things. Someday Teddy will be better, but right now he needs you. You can't be yellin' at him every time he messes up."

"He never listens," I groused. Teddy had returned to his curled-up spot on the pallet. His shoulders were shaking as he cried silently. He hated it when I was cross with him.

"He does when he can. And sometimes he just can't, bud." Benny's voice was nearly a whisper.

"What do you mean?"

Benny coughed for several seconds. It came from deep in his lungs and didn't sound good. I wondered if he'd breathed in too much smoke or something.

"What I mean is . . . a man goes through somethin'. Every time he sees a horrible thing it changes him. Some can handle it. You're one of those men. But others ain't never gonna be able to. Teddy can do things. He just can't do *this*. It don't mean he's weak or a bad person or nothin' like that. I seen it all the time while I been traveling around the Pacific, teaching Hirohito some manners and other such duties as assigned."

Benny coughed again and his scrawny shoulders shook. He finally stopped and moaned in pain. His condition was starting to worry me.

"There was this guy in my unit in basic trainin', big dude outta Cleveland named Kolar. Strong as a bull and the most squared-away marine you're ever gonna see. All during those hot days at Camp Pendleton, this guy could chew up iron and spit out nails."

Benny coughed again. I gave him a small sip of water from the canteen. Even his tongue was burned as it darted out of his mouth, and he licked his cracked and bleeding lips.

"Thanks, bud," he said. "Anyway, Kolar practically danced through basic while the rest of us was suckin' wind. Graduated with higher scores than anybody. Then we ship out for Guadalcanal. We hit the beach in the first wave of the landin' and the Imperial Japanese Army is layin' down so much machine gun fire you could have walked on bullets all the way up and shook their hands. I lost half'a my platoon before we even made it to the sand. And what does Kolar do?"

"I don't know, Benny, what did he do?"

"I tell you what he did. He makes it onto the beach, but once he's there, he curls up behind this log, don't ever fire his weapon, and stays there screaming like a wounded donkey until we turned Hirohito's ground pounders into mincemeat and the shootin' was over."

"I don't understand, Benny," I said. "What does that have to do with me and Teddy?"

"What I'm sayin' is, some of us can handle things and some of us can't. Tough things, bad things. We find somethin' inside ourselves, somethin' that makes it possible for us to just keep on goin'. We do what needs to be done. But Teddy ain't like you. He can't survive this without his brother helpin' him. That's why you got to watch out for him. Kolar weren't a bad guy. He weren't even a coward. He just found what his limit was. Teddy is done gone past his limit, poor kid. But when the two of you get back to Dee-troit, he's gonna find his thing that he can do that you can't. The thing in the world what makes him special. It might be music. Or he invents a flyin' car. It might even be he grows up and takes over for that bum, Greenberg, in left field. Until then, you gotta do the things he can't do for him. We're marines. We don't leave no man behind, *capisce*? No matter how hard it gets or how mad he makes ya. Right now, you're the only thing Teddy has got in this world."

"I guess," I sighed.

"I didn't say it would be easy, sport."

I reached out and touched Teddy on the back. After a moment he stopped crying and shaking. While Teddy calmed down I told Benny what had happened with Colosi. He was instantly angry.

"That jamoke is lucky I was unconscious, or he'd

have been given a quick lesson in what's what. That's a lead-pipe cinch," Benny muttered. "Are you okay, kid?"

"Yeah," I said. "I mean, I was scared and all. But maybe it's like you said. Maybe Colosi just reached his limit. Maybe he was just trying to survive. Like we all are."

"Maybe. Still don't give nobody the right to beat up on a defenseless kid."

"I whacked him pretty good, Benny. I'm not defenseless."

That made Benny laugh. "You sure ain't, sport. You're about the least defenseless twelve-year-old I ever met."

The moon was sinking in the sky. As it dropped farther, the wind rose and came whistling across the surface of the water. Not long after that, the waves started up again, the pallet lifting and falling as it floated along.

"Patty boy, listen," Benny said. "The seas is gettin' rough again. You gotta wake Teddy up, and you boys find a way to tie yourselves to this pallet. Use your belts. We don't need nobody fallin' off in the dark."

I looked around at the water's surface. The waves were a couple of feet high and getting bigger. We had been in a debris field earlier, and I wondered if maybe there was something floating by we could use. The only thing I found was a piece of wood about three feet long and four inches wide. I managed to snatch it from the water. I kept scanning the water's surface hoping to find a piece of rope, a strap or netting, anything, but the only thing I saw made me shrink back in fear.

"Benny, we got worse problems," I said.

"What is it, sport?"

"The sharks are back. The big ones."

First one, then two—then five—large, dark dorsal fins popped out of the water, slowly circling the raft.

CHAPTER ELEVEN

SEA OF FEAR

★ ★ ★

We're just gonna stay calm and quiet, and I bet they don't even notice us," Benny said.

Calm. Who could stay calm? So far we were lucky that Teddy was asleep again. I didn't think it was possible to sleep as much as Teddy did. But now I was glad of it. If he'd seen the sharks, he might've gone all crazy again. I knew Benny was right. I needed to be more patient with him. But sometimes it drove me flippin' nuts.

"Patrick, you gotta listen to me. Take your belt off and tie you and Teddy to the raft! I would lend you a hand, but..." Benny held up his gnarled, burned hands and tried to laugh, but ended up having a coughing fit. He couldn't stop.

"Benny?" I gently made my way to his side. The pallet rocked and swayed, but finally he stopped and cleared his lungs.

"Benny?" I repeated.

"Yeah, kid."

"Tell me the truth. Are you all right?" I supposed that large group of floating men was out there somewhere, but they were simply too far away to be of any help to us now. With only the occasional sliver of moonlight it was clear there was no one around us. It made any thought of getting Benny to the doctor out of the question. For now at least.

"I'm fine, sport. I ain't sayin' I'm gonna dance the jitterbug right away, but as soon as we get plucked outta the drink, we're gonna find your parents, and then I'm goin' back to givin' Tojo and his samurai jokers a double dose of United States marine. Now, stop screwin' around and get your belts—"

The raft shook and a loud crack startled us both. Behind us, one of the sharks bit off a chunk of the pallet and split several of the remaining boards in the process. It must have sensed the pallet shaking from

Benny's coughing, and while I wasn't paying attention it slithered through the water to investigate. And now it was practically lying on top of the wood with us. Teddy woke in an instant. He scrambled to his knees and backed away from the giant beast. He pointed at it and started crying. Between gasping breaths he keened louder than ever. I worried it'd rile the shark up.

"Teddy," I hissed. "Quiet down. For the love of God, be quiet."

But he couldn't stop. He was terrified.

"Patrick, you gotta be careful, but you need to make him stop. Ease your way over to him and see if you can keep him quiet. I think the noise is what's drawin' the sharks. Right now he sounds like a wounded seal or somethin'."

The shark was still there chewing away at the boards, shaking its head. Then it paused for a moment. Its tail swished back and forth, but its head was still and it stared straight at me.

I looked at its dead eyes. For a brief second I wondered what it saw. Did a shark see a world outside of the ocean? Did it see me a few feet away, kneeling next to an injured marine, my brother screaming like a banshee? Was it trying to decide which one of us it was going to eat next? Or was it blind out of the water?

"Patrick," Benny said quietly. "Go to Teddy and take your stick. You gotta get him to quiet down."

I sat frozen. It felt like time had stopped. The shark backed into the water and then lunged forward again, tearing at the pallet. I didn't want to move. If I moved, it would see me. But I also wanted Teddy to shut up.

"Patrick," Benny coaxed. "You got a wounded man on the field. You gotta go get 'em. Come on, now."

On my knees, I slowly inched my way toward Teddy. I picked up the board I'd found in the water. Teddy was rocking back and forth, shaking the pallet, which seemed to be exciting the shark. The great beast opened its mouth and its eyes turned from dark to white, as if they had rolled up in its head. When its jaws snapped shut, the noise sounded like a gunshot.

To make matters worse, the waves were getting higher. The pallet was bobbing up and down, making it hard to keep my balance. I reached out and touched Teddy on the shoulder, but he jerked away.

"Teddy, hush," I said. "You need to be quiet."

"Aah! Aah!"

The shark slipped back in the water, its tail whipping the water into a foamy froth. I hustled the rest of the way to Teddy and put my arm around his shoulder. I knew the shark was coming back any second. But Teddy fought me, wiggling away, screaming and pointing.

"Yeah, Teddy, I see there's a shark. It might go away if you're quiet. So let's be quiet, okay?"

The shark didn't like the taste of the wood, but it appeared to sense it was near food. It lunged forward again, its giant jaws snapping shut. I threw one arm around Teddy and clutched the board in my hand. I needed Teddy to calm down. And with both of us so close to each other, I needed to distribute our weight so the pallet wouldn't drop us into the sea. Where this shark's buddies were just waiting to claim its leftovers.

"Teddy! Teddy! Bad guys come! Bad guys come! Down!" I shouted as I tried to balance the pallet.

Teddy's eyes grew wide and he stopped mid-scream. Back on Guam, living with the Chamorro guerrilla band in the jungles, a man everyone called Iggy was in charge. I don't know what his real name was or how you pronounced it exactly. But Iggy was the leader and probably the one most responsible for keeping us alive as we crisscrossed the island, dodging Japanese patrols. Whenever they were nearby, Iggy would say "Bad guys come." Instantly we would get down low and quietly melt into the underbrush. Teddy learned to recognize those words. It was the only thing that'd reliably make him be silent. Iggy kept us alive until the American forces retook the island. He died fighting during the worst of the battle. I never got a chance to thank him for keeping us safe.

It worked now. Teddy stopped yelling, knelt down, and buried his head in my arms.

"That's good, Patty boy," Benny whispered. "Real good. Now let's all be still, and we'll be out of this mess soon."

It was getting darker by the minute, and difficult to see, but the shark was still there. It thrashed in the water just a few feet away. We waited and waited as the seconds ticked by.

"Be still now, fellas," Benny said. "That old fish is gonna amscray soon."

Teddy was getting restless, starting to moan and wiggle in my arms.

"Shhh, Teddy. Bad guys come. Bad guys come. Shh," I whispered in his ear.

But I was wrong, because this time it wasn't the Japanese attacking. It was the shark. Without warning, it launched itself forward.

"Watch it, boys! Look out!" Benny yelled.

The shark flew through the water and landed with a loud smack on the pallet. More of the boards cracked, and the shark's jaws snapped as it thrashed its head back and forth looking for something to bite. It was huge. At least fifteen feet long. And its weight pushed the pallet below the water's surface.

"Hold on! Grab hold!" Benny shouted. "We can't lose it."

I held Teddy around his waist and grabbed the pallet with my hand. The weight of the shark pushed it under the water until we were submerged up to our waists. Then the shark flopped onto its side and slid across the surface of the pallet toward the two of us.

"Watch out, Patrick!" Benny screamed.

As the giant shark's body collided with Teddy and me, its hard, sharp skin cut my arms. I tried to hang on to the pallet, but the weight of the shark was too much for me.

Teddy and I tumbled into the sea.

CHAPTER TWELVE

FRENZY

★ ★ ★

Teddy and I thrashed underwater, our limbs colliding as we tried to right ourselves. I couldn't see anything, most importantly the shark. Grabbing Teddy's arm, I kicked to the surface, pulling him with me.

"Benny!" I hollered as loud as I could.

"I'm here, pipsqueak! I'm right over here!" he answered back.

I spun around in the water looking for him. But the waves were too big. I didn't see Benny or our raft anywhere.

"Where?!" I shouted.

Teddy was clutching my back and dragging me under. We resurfaced and I shouted at him.

"Teddy, you gotta settle down or we're both going to drown," I yelled. I tried prying his arms from around my neck, but he had a grip like iron. The only thing I could think to do was to duck beneath the water, pulling him with me. I held my breath and waited, making sure I didn't sink too far.

Teddy still struggled and thrashed, trying to hold on to me, but his instinct for survival finally won out and he shot upward. I came up sputtering behind him and grabbed him loosely around the neck.

"You got to kick your legs, Teddy, so we can tread water. We need to find Benny and get back on the raft," I said.

I didn't have to worry about Teddy kicking his legs. He was wild with fear. He spun about like a maniac. It kept us above the water, but it also brought us an unwanted visitor.

"Patrick!" Benny shouted again.

His voice was coming from somewhere behind me. I turned, holding Teddy with my left arm, and no more than ten feet away was a shark coming at us with its mouth wide open. This close, its teeth looked like daggers. Its jaws yawned even wider, its mouth looked big enough to swallow the two of us whole. It came closer, and all I could focus on was the way its teeth gleamed with bright white menace against its dark skin.

I still had the board in my right hand and I swung it with all the strength I could muster. It hit the shark square on its gills. The beast seemed to bristle and dove beneath us, the rough surface of its skin scraping against my legs. I could barely see it, only the tail slicing through the water's surface. And now it was somewhere below. The sky was dark now, and cloudy. What kind of place was this? The sun burns all day and at night you get clouds covering up the moon so you can't even see.

"Benny!"

If he answered, I couldn't hear him over the sound of waves, wind, and my shrieking brother.

Two more fins popped up out of the water, slowly circling us. They were just out of reach of my weapon, such as it was. Teddy thrashed and struggled, so I pulled him onto his back, my arm looped over his left shoulder and under his right arm. I had to stop him from attracting their attention.

"Teddy!" I shouted. "Take a deep breath and hold it. It will help us hide," I whispered in his ear. For once, he did what I told him. I did the same and floated on my back, supporting Teddy by letting him rest on top of me. We let the waves carry us. But the sharks kept circling. I wondered if they could smell the blood from my cuts.

We let our breath out slowly and started to sink. The big fish were yet to make a move toward us. "Take another breath, Teddy," I whispered. "The Japanese are close." Teddy sucked in a great lungful of air. We held our breath and floated again while the sharks sized us up.

Every instinct told me to shout out for Benny. But I had this feeling that if I did, the sharks would attack. And I might set Teddy off again. The thought of holding our breath throughout the night and beyond was not something I was looking forward to. But it beat dying.

Soon, more fins appeared. Now there were sharks

all around us. There was no way for me to keep my eye on all of them.

"Teddy," I whispered. "We're in the jungle now. Hiding in the underbrush just like with Iggy. Those dark things, those are the enemy. You watch the front and I'll watch the back, and if you see them coming, you say so. You shout out and Iggy will shoot it. Nod your head if you understand me."

Teddy took another deep breath and nodded. I turned him until we were floating back-to-back in the water. As we held our breath, I hooked my left arm through Teddy's right arm. I held the short board in my right hand. In my mind, I sat in the stands at Briggs Stadium with my dad. I closed my eyes and saw Hank Greenberg stepping up to the plate, his spikes digging into the dirt. I saw the pitcher wind up and release the ball. Then I saw Hammerin' Hank take that sweet swing, the ball jumping off the bat, rifling its way through the air and over the wall. The sharks were the baseball. The board was my Louisville Slugger. If any shark came near us, it was going to get a quick lesson in how a kid from Detroit, Michigan, could fight. If we were going down, we were going down swinging. I didn't know another way to be. I wouldn't just give in. Benny said there were people looking for us. We were going to make it out of here. All of us. Or my name wasn't Patrick James O'Donnell of Detroit, Michigan.

The smallest of the group slowly swam toward me. I guess it could smell the blood on my legs after all. I twisted us around so that Teddy was behind me. Closer and closer it came. Its nose was blunt and square, and it slowed its approach as it drew nearer. The shape of its head made it hard for me to get the right angle to hit it in the gills. The other sharks just kept circling us.

I figured if I popped it square on the nose now, I'd just make it angrier. But I wanted to be ready, just in case, so I lifted the board out of the water. I noticed that my arm was covered in blood and the dark sludge of diesel fuel. We must have hit another patch of it. But even though I was bleeding more than I'd thought, the smallest shark just sort of hovered two feet away. It didn't attack us, and neither did its friends. Maybe it was like Benny had said. We were small and they were looking for something more than an appetizer.

Back home, our next-door neighbors, the Moselys, had a dog. His name was Brewster and he was a friendly mutt. Teddy and I liked playing with him. Every day, when we came home from school, Brewster would come bounding over from the Mosleys's yard to greet us. The first thing he would do was sniff our legs, hands, and arms, really checking us out, to see if we smelled like anything interesting.

It was like the shark was doing the same thing. Teddy and I were holding our breath and floating along. As long as we didn't kick or splash, the sharks acted like curious dogs more interested in smelling us than eating us.

"Teddy, you keep an eye out," I said. "If one comes near, you let me know."

I must not have had a very interesting scent, because the shark in front of me took one last look, then dove beneath the surface and was gone. It was no cause for celebration. The others hadn't gone anywhere. I couldn't shout out for Benny. I was afraid the noise would bring them after us. Now I worried that Benny and the pallet had been carried away from us on the current. Would this be how we would spend the night? How we would die? A standoff where we tried to be quiet and the sharks waited for us to make a single sound, as if that were permission to finish us off?

"Aah! Aah!" Teddy shouted, pulling me back from my morbid thoughts. I jerked around to look, and found one of the sharks swimming toward him along the surface of the water. I pushed him behind me, and as the shark lunged forward, I swung the board down on its snout as hard as I could. With a great thwack, the board splintered in half lengthwise. It was like fighting a dinosaur with a toothpick.

One of the broken pieces spun out of my hands. But the piece I was left with had a sharp point. The shark shook its head as if it was confused, then angled toward me. I jabbed the sharp edge of the stick at its eye. The shark didn't back down, but I didn't, either. I kept stabbing at it as it stared out at me with cold, soulless eyes. It looked like a robot from one of the science fiction comics we bought at Kresge's. All it was designed to do was eat.

"Get away!" I shouted. "Get away from us!"

I stabbed at it again and scored a direct hit on its eye with the pointed end of the stick.

"Leave us alone!"

"Aah, aah!" Teddy had lost his concentration. He kicked and screamed and thrashed in the water. We had nothing to lose, so I shouted and kicked with him. I hit the shark in the eye again, and it peeled away. But the noise was now drawing the attention of the other sharks, and they veered toward us.

"Hang on, Teddy!" I said. "Hang on! I won't let them get you! Don't worry, buddy! You're the best bro—"

A large wave rose up behind the sharks, and there came Benny on the pallet. It hit the water with a loud smack, right between the onrushing sharks, who were startled by its unexpected appearance.

"Get up here, boys! Hurry!" Benny shouted. The sharks turned tail and swam away, but I was pretty sure they would be coming back. I grabbed Teddy and put his foot in my cupped hands to boost him up onto the pallet.

"Help me, Teddy," I said. I wasn't sure I had the strength to make it up. Teddy just sat there, not moving, curled up on his side. Benny scooted over and held out his arm. I couldn't take his hand. It was too badly burned. He couldn't lift me. I finally found the strength to clamber up the rest of the way.

The waves lifted the raft again and it slammed down on the water's surface. I rolled over onto my back.

"How did you find us?" I said.

"Told you," Benny said. "Marines don't leave no man behind."

CHAPTER THIRTEEN

NIGHT TERRORS

★ ★ ★

31 JULY 1945

That night, I was the most scared I've ever been in my life. I'd been frightened many times in the jungle. Before we left for Manila, Dad took us to see Bela Lugosi in a double feature of *The Phantom Creeps* and *Son of Frankenstein* at the Fox Theatre. I still remembered how much I jumped when the son of Frankenstein appeared on the screen and how Dad had chuckled at me, but not too much—because he jumped, too. I spent most of that night scared out of my wits. But Hollywood monsters were nothing compared to real live sharks with a taste for blood.

I still don't know how we survived the onslaught. The pallet was waterlogged and coming apart, especially at the big gash down the middle. It creaked and moaned as it was tossed about by the waves. The noise must have attracted more sharks, because they were constantly attacking and knocking against it. After one visit by a fifteen-foot tiger shark, another one of the boards snapped. It hung loosely, attached only by a single nail. I managed to pry it off the pallet, with the nail still sticking out of the end, and used it to poke and club the sharks away. For some reason the nail made me feel better. I had an actual weapon. But I knew I was just getting slaphappy from lack of sleep and water. A nail? Against sharks three times my size. Yes. That would work. Since I didn't happen to have a cannon lying around.

Benny lay in the middle of the raft with Teddy huddled next to him. Benny couldn't hold on to him and keep him secure on the pallet, as he would have liked, because of his burned hands. But he did his best to comfort him with soothing words and even the occasional song.

Several times, when enough moonlight shone through the clouds, I spied the bodies of dozens of dead sailors floating by in the waves. They bobbed in the water, rising and falling to the rhythm of the ocean swells. And even when the seas turned rough, it didn't matter. Not to them. They didn't have to worry about anything anymore.

Hours passed and finally the waves calmed. When the clouds parted for a moment, the moonlight revealed one of the dead men floating close to our pallet. He wore a life jacket and clutched another in his hand. I wanted them. Teddy could have one, and Benny and I could share the other. It'd give me one less thing to worry about. And they were right there, just a few feet away.

But they weren't close enough to reach. I slid closer to the edge of the pallet, as far as I dared without falling in the water. I set the nail stick down, grabbed hold of one of the pallet's wooden slats, and leaned out over the water. I hoped that for once the sea would be on my side, that the waves would push the loose life jacket closer. Nothing doing. So I grabbed the nail stick and extended my arm as far as I could.

There was no way I was going in the water, not even for a life jacket. I knew the sharks were there, even though I couldn't see them. Instead, I stretched and strained, trying to reach it with my stick. My arms shook, but I couldn't stop trying. With one last effort, I hooked the nail over one of the straps. Success! I pulled it toward me and sat back up on the raft.

Just as I was about to yank it onto the pallet, I heard a sharp intake of breath. The water exploded in a flurry of splashing foam. Was it another shark? I needed my arm more than I needed the life jacket, so I jerked backward, losing my balance and nearly tumbling over the side.

"Lemme go! Lemme go!" Who was yelling? Benny and Teddy hadn't moved from their spot on the pallet. Then I realized the strangled voice was coming from the dead sailor. Only, he wasn't dead. He was alive and thrashing.

"Stop! You've got to calm down!" I pleaded, willing him to settle himself before he attracted the sharks.

"Get away! You get away from me!"

"Okay, all right! Just relax," I begged him. I let go of the life jacket. He pulled it back into the water with him.

"Who are you?" he demanded.

"I'm just a survivor," I said. "Like you."

"I don't know you. What'd you do to Litkowski?"

"I don't know any Litkowski," I said.

"Liar. I saw you. I saw what you did." He'd let go of me and was treading water furiously.

"I don't know what you think you saw, but I didn't do anything to Lit—" The sailor lunged toward me, thrashing and kicking, the water foaming around him. I swung my nail stick and hit him on the wrist.

"Ow! Why would you do that . . . and where's Litkowski?"

"I don't know. I'm sorry I bothered you, mister. I thought . . . I thought . . . you had . . . You were float-ing there and not moving and I figured you were . . . had passed . . . I'm sorry." I didn't know what to say. I'd been about to strip the poor man of his life jackets. Now he was alive and obviously quite delirious.

"I ain't dead. I ain't!" he said.

"I can see that," I said. "But I sure wish you would settle down. These waters are full of sharks and—"

"No sharks! No! Litkowski said no sharks would get me. But you killed him. You killed him!" he grew agitated again, thrusting his arms back and forth in the water.

"Sailor, tell me your name," I said.

"You want Litkowski's life jacket? Because you killed him!" He tossed it high, and I watched it spin wildly through the air and land several yards away. There would be no way for me to retrieve it without diving in now.

"Let me help you," I suggested. "You can grab hold of our raft and drift along with us until we get rescued." In truth, I didn't want him anywhere near us, but I hoped the offer would calm him down. It had the opposite effect.

"Oh you'd like that, wouldn't you? You'd get rid of me, just like you did Litkowski," he said. He tugged at the straps on his life jacket. He was taking it off.

"Sailor," I said. "Don't do that. You need to keep that jacket on!"

There was no stopping him. For several minutes I pleaded with him as he worked the knots loose. He raved about Litkowski, becoming more and more unhinged with each passing moment. "Me and Litkowski are a team. Brothers. What did you do to him? If he doesn't have one of these, I won't have one." He shrugged out of the vest and swam over to the one he'd tossed. He shot me a dirty look and ripped into them with his teeth like a rabid dog. He barely seemed human anymore. Was that what would happen to all of us eventually? Did this endless sea make everything in it turn crazy?

"Mister, don't do that! You gotta put it back on! Please!" I said. I watched as he massacred those life vests. They weren't going to do anything for anyone now. "Please, just come float with us. We're going to get rescued."

Something changed in him then. He looked me right in the eye and his expression grew calm. "We *aren't* going to get rescued. Litkowski said so. He said the ship exploded. They never had time to get the distress call out. We're all alone. All alone."

"You don't know that! A plane or ship could come along at any minute. You have to hold on. Please swim over and get that life jacket and—"

"No," he said calmly. "I'm going to get Litkowski. He'll know what to do."

He gave me one last look, then sunk beneath the waves with the tattered life jackets clutched in his fists.

CHAPTER FOURTEEN

BUT A DREAM

★ ★ ★

I didn't want to lose myself like the poor man who just gave up and sank below the water. I couldn't get the image out of my mind. I tried, but it was hot and I was thirsty and tired. Soon my mind was playing tricks on me. I slept and woke, and slept and woke. I couldn't remember if this was the second or third or how many days we'd been in the water. I think we passed a whole day if not more, just baking in the sun on the raft, but I couldn't be sure. None of us had a watch. Teddy was delirious and Benny spent most of the time groaning in pain and sleeping fitfully.

Maybe it was exhaustion or dehydration or hunger, but I started seeing strange things in the water. One time I heard Mom and Dad calling my name. I looked behind me and there they were, heading straight toward the raft in a powerful, sleek motorboat, like the ones we used to watch zip up and down the Detroit River.

"Patrick! Teddy!" My mom called from the boat. My dad was at the wheel. Mom looked like she was dressed for a picnic, in a bright yellow blouse. Dad was wearing a straw hat and a floral-print Hawaiian shirt. They looked like they'd just stepped out of an advertisement in a magazine. I was so happy to see them.

"Mom!" I shouted. "Mom, we're right over here! I did it, Mom. I took care of Teddy, just like you said!"

"I know you did, sweetheart! I know you did! I'm so proud of you!"

"Will you come get us?" I shouted back across the water.

"We sure will, but I need you to do one more thing first."

I groaned. After all this time, I just wanted to get in the boat with my parents. And they were giving me chores?

"What, Mom? What is it you want me to do?"

"Look out for the shark!" she yelled.

"Wha . . . Mom . . . what?!"

Yet another shark hammered into the side of the pallet, jolting me out of my stupor. Benny woke up and unleashed a loud stream of curse words. Teddy just wailed and buried his head in his arms.

The shark had maneuvered its way right into the V-shape of the pallet. It moved quicker than I could, and soon its snapping jaws were inches away from my face. I screamed and swung my nail-topped stick at it with all my might and hit it right in the gills. It thrashed its head back and forth but wasn't giving up the fight. This shark was big. Maybe the largest one we'd seen. And with its size and strength and the fuss it was making, it split the raft in two before deciding we weren't worth the trouble and sinking beneath the water.

"Patty boy!" Benny called, as a wave spun Teddy and him around. Within seconds they were drifting away from me.

Lightning fast, I swung the nail stick like a hammer. The nail stuck in the wooden surface of their half of the raft. With every ounce of strength I had left, I pulled them back toward me, until I could grab hold.

"Quick thinkin' there, pipsqueak," Benny said. "But like I told you earlier, you gotta take off your belt, and Teddy's, too, and tie us to one another. I don't want to have to bust you for not followin' orders."

I did as he instructed and managed to lash the pallet back together, stopping only once to beat back another shark that attacked us. I did it without even thinking too much this time. *I suppose I'm getting used to the beasts*, I thought as my stomach rumbled. I was so, so hungry. And I guessed the sharks were, too. I couldn't blame them for trying to find a meal. I just wouldn't let them succeed.

"Good job, marine," Benny said as I tied the second belt in place. "Your ship is secure. By the way, a ship needs a name. What are you going to call your vessel, Captain? How about the USS *Iron Horse*?"

I shook my head.

"The USS *Greenberg*."

"That ain't even funny," Benny said.

All night long, the sharks kept coming. Only now that I understood them, I made sure they understood me. They bothered us, but none came close to doing any real damage. Then, just as the sun was about to crest the horizon in the east, they started getting testy. Long ones, short ones, really aggressive ones, all seemed desperate to feed before the rising heat of the day. They reminded me of the Japanese arriving back on Guam, how they just kept coming at us relentlessly. Between holding on to the raft in the violent waves and clubbing, kicking, and screaming at sharks all night, I was completely spent. When the sun rose and the water calmed, I lay there, flat on my back, the jagged wooden planks cutting into my shoulder blades. I didn't think I would ever be able to move again.

It was now dawn. The pallet was saturated and sinking. It floated a few inches below the surface. Every cut and scrape on our bodies was swelling, and the salt water made them burn with unending pain. The sun hurt my eyes. Even screwed shut, the harsh light penetrated through my eyelids. Groaning with the effort,

I threw my arm across my face to cut the glare and give myself some relief.

It was clear to me now that no one was looking for us. The distress call hadn't gone out. We'd only seen a few of the other survivors since that first morning. What if everyone else had been found and rescued, but no one found us? What if they'd left us here to die? The thought made me angry. Angry with the men who might have gotten the help we so desperately needed, with the navy who hadn't been able to stop the torpedo or save the *Indy*, with Benny for helping us get on the ship in the first place, with Teddy for acting the way he did, and most of all with myself for ever thinking I could find my parents. What a fool I was.

I had read newspapers and heard reports of what happened after the Japanese landed in the Philippines. Of course my mom and dad had never made it out of there on the next plane. If they had, and the plane made it to safety, they would have found us. I knew they'd been stuck in Manila during the invasion, or I never would have gotten on that ship. But in my heart, I suspected they weren't waiting for us. The Japanese army had ravaged Guam. Why wouldn't they do the same in the Philippines? My parents had probably been shot or taken to a camp. They were most likely dead.

A fool. That's what I was.

It took tremendous effort to turn my head. Lifting my arm I looked at Benny, really looked at him for the first time since he'd come back to the hold to get us after the explosions. His hands and forearms looked even worse than I'd remembered, and I wondered if a shark had gotten hold of him while I was sleeping and I'd missed it. But probably the burns were just getting worse without treatment. His skin was blistered and flaking and chunks of it were coming off. His fingers had curled up and were digging into the palms of his hands. His face was sunken and cracked. His shirt had torn away, revealing dozens of white, puckered scars on his back. I wondered if he'd gotten those in the fighting on Guam. I knew he'd been injured, but he never really liked to talk about that. Poor Benny had been through a lot.

Teddy shook in his sleep. He was sunburnt and his lips were split and swollen. A layer of oily sludge covered us all. I guess that's what happens when you spend days floating through the patches of diesel fuel that spread out over the ocean surface like spilled paint. Seeing Teddy and Benny in such rough shape made me wonder what I looked like. I wanted a drink of water so badly. The sound of the lapping waves against the wood drove me nearly mad with thirst. My tongue was swollen and like Teddy, my lips were cracked and bleeding. The inside of my mouth was completely dry. I tried to wet my lips, but it was like licking steel wool.

The temperature rose as the sun lifted higher in the sky. I would have given my right eye for a cloudy, overcast day like the night the ship went down. The sun warmed the water near the surface, so even it provided no relief from the unrelenting heat. With a groan, I pulled myself up to sit. I was staring at the horizon when something bumped against the pallet. *Not again, I can't take any more,* I thought. But it wasn't a shark.

It was a turnip.

It floated on the surface of the ocean like a bobber attached to a fishing line. My muscles screamed at me as I leaned over on my side and plucked it out of the water. It took considerable effort, but I sat back up so I could inspect it.

The turnip was dirty and covered in oily sludge. I tried finding a clean spot on my shirt to wipe it off, but there wasn't one, so I had to settle for the least greasy. It was an honest-to-goodness turnip. A vegetable. I hated turnips, but right then it looked like the most delicious, juiciest fruit I'd ever seen. I couldn't believe that we'd finally had a little luck.

"Teddy, Benny." My voice was a sorry-sounding croak. "We got food." Neither of them moved. I wiped more grease off the turnip with my fingers and took a bite. It tasted salty and bitter, but I choked it down. I bit off another piece. Whatever moisture was inside the turnip was nearly gone, and my tongue burned, but I swallowed another huge chunk.

"Benny, Teddy, wake up," I said. "I found a turnip."

They didn't stir. They were so exhausted that not even the promise of food could rouse them. I took one more bite, resisting the urge to eat the entire thing. I needed to save some of it for Benny and Teddy.

Then my stomach rumbled. I was so hungry, but maybe eating hadn't been a good idea. Suddenly sick, I twisted over the side of the pallet and retched, chunks of greasy, salty turnip rising up in my throat and spewing into the water. My stomach cramped and I clutched it with one arm, but the other wouldn't surrender the dirty vegetable back to the ocean. With my stomach empty, I fell back on the pallet.

I'm not sure how long I lay there. When I came to, the sun was high in the sky, so it must have been midday. My stomach still hurt and the inside of my mouth stung like heck. But I sat up anyway and scanned the horizon.

Far off in the distance, I saw something moving. At first I thought it was just another shark. But it didn't have the right shape. The more I studied it, the more I was sure that it wasn't a fish or any kind of sea creature. And it was headed in our direction.

After about a half hour, it was even closer. I tried shouting, "Hello," but all that came out was a sickly-sounding rasp. I was sure whoever or whatever it was couldn't hear me.

The weird noises I was making finally roused Benny, and he looked up at me.

"What's up, pipsqueak?" His voice barely carried over the noise of the waves.

"There's something out there, headed this way," I said. "I think it might be men from the ship. Also, I found a turnip. I tried to wake you both, but you wouldn't get up. I took two bites and threw up. I think the salt water ruined it."

"No kiddin'," he said. "That's a lot to happen while a guy is sleepin'." He tried to follow my gaze to look off at the approaching object but couldn't manage to move. "If it's guys from the ship, maybe we can get a poker game goin'."

The joke was funny, but I didn't have the energy to laugh. Another half an hour later, I could finally make out the approaching shape. It was four men covered in diesel fuel, and they all looked like they'd seen better days. One of them had been burned on the side of the face, only not as bad as Benny. The others were all sporting various injuries.

When they were no more than fifty yards away, I recognized one of them. It was difficult at first, with their faces so grimy. But I saw the stripes on his sleeve. It was Sergeant Stenkevitz, the guy Benny had argued with when he was helping us stow away. And it looked like he was the only one of the four left alive.

When they came closer, it was clear that the other three men were definitely corpses. Their heads hung limply against their chests. They had lashed themselves together back-to-back with the extra straps on the life jackets and formed a human raft. To keep an eye out for sharks, I guessed. Now, it was a pretty gruesome vessel, as Stenkevitz floated along with his three dead companions. Like the pallet we were using, the life jackets were waterlogged. They wouldn't keep him afloat much longer.

"Who are you?" Stenkevitz demanded.

"Patrick O'Donnell," I said.

"What are you doing out here?"

"We were on the ship. The *Indianapolis*."

"Who else is that with you?"

Something about the way Stenkevitz was acting made me uneasy. His eyes were wild and they darted everywhere. When he talked, they kind of rolled back in his head. It was strange.

"Who you got with you? I asked you a question!" he said. He was hoarse and his words sounded choked off in his mouth.

"Just a couple of guys from the ship," I said. I figured it wasn't a good idea for him to know Benny was here. Stenkevitz already had it in for him. And why was Benny sitting still for this? I looked over at him to find he was unconscious again.

"A couple . . . ? That one is shaking. He don't look so good."

"No, they're just passed out."

"My crew is dead. Why ain't you wearing a uniform?"

I didn't know what to say. If by some miracle we were rescued, I still didn't want Benny getting in trouble. Stenkevitz stared at me. Waiting for an answer.

"I . . . uh . . . just . . . when . . . I just came off leave and didn't have a chance to change before . . ."

I don't have any idea where it came from, but in the next instant he was pointing a pistol at me. I'd learned a lot about weapons from the Chamorro, and I recognized it as a .45 caliber automatic. Most US military personnel carried one. It was a big, powerful handgun. And it looked much bigger and more powerful when it was pointed at you.

"Wrong answer," he said.

"What? No . . . I'm not your enemy," I said.

"I think you are. I think you and some of your Imperial Navy buddies snuck aboard my ship and blew it up. Probably because you two . . ."

Benny groaned and woke up.

"What's going on, sport?" he asked. His voice was so weak I could barely hear him.

"Shh, Benny, we got a little problem," I said.

"Who you talking to?" Stenkevitz demanded, waving the pistol at me. "Is this some kind of trick?"

"I'm not talking to anyone," I said. "And I'm not your enemy."

"That's exactly what a lousy Japanese-loving traitor *would* say, you lying sneak. Why are you waiting out here? For a sub to come along and pick you up?"

"We're not Japanese sailors. We were on the *Indianapolis* when it blew up, just like you were," I said.

"Who is that?" Benny said in his whispery voice.

"It's Stenkevitz," I said. "He thinks we're in the Japanese navy and we sunk the ship."

Benny snorted. "Well, then Admiral Yamamoto has got to command the sorriest navy in the entire Pacific theater if they'd let us in, the shape we're in. Stenkevitz ain't exactly what you'd call a genius."

"He's got a gun," I said quietly.

"He what?" Benny wheezed.

"Who you talkin' to?" Stenkevitz demanded. "You got a radio? Trying to call your Japanese navy buddies?"

He raised the gun and pointed it at me.

"I'm not talking to the Japanese navy," I said. "And be careful with that gun."

"Give me your radio!" Stenkevitz said.

"Patty boy?" Benny whispered. "He's hallucinatin'. Be careful."

"I don't have a radio," I said.

"Liar! I see it right there in your hand! Give it to me!" Stenkevitz yelled.

He was about ten yards from the pallet now. At this distance, the gun looked like a cannon. And the sergeant had gone crazy enough to fire it. I don't know why he thought I had a radio. I looked down. In my right hand, I held the board with the nail through the end, which wouldn't do me any good—he was too far away. In my other hand I still clutched the turnip. Could he possibly think it was a radio?

"This? This isn't a radio, it's a turnip," I said holding it up.

Stenkevitz shook his head. "You stinking little— you give me that radio. Hand it over now!"

"All right. All right. Take it easy," I said.

"Toss it over here! Do you hear me?" The more he talked, the worse his voice got.

I flung the turnip toward him, but I was so weak that it only made it about half the distance to Stenkevitz

149

before it flopped into the water. It floated there between the pallet and Stenkevitz and the dead men. Slowly, his face turned from wild-eyed hysteria to burning anger.

"You little yel . . . You did that on purpose!"

"No! I didn't! Don't shoot! You don't understand, I've been out here for days now, fighting off sharks and . . ."

"Sharks? Where's a shark?" Stenkevitz said, instantly terrified. His head swiveled around, looking in every direction.

This was my chance. Yes, I was weak, but I was also determined. Stenkovitz was not going to shoot me. Not when I'd managed to survive everything else. I concentrated, cocked my arm, and threw my nail stick at Stenkevitz like a tomahawk. It twirled through the air, whirling end over end until it thumped into the side of his head.

"Ow!" he shouted in pain. His hands instinctively went up to soothe his temple, and he dropped the gun. It sank into the water before he could do anything to stop it. I only hoped he didn't have another one hidden in the folds of his "life raft."

"You rotten little stinking . . . you . . . I'll kill you!" he screamed. "You hear me? I'll kill you!"

Benny had been floating in and out of consciousness. "What just happened? What'd you do?" he asked me.

"I gave him a tap on the conk. Threw my stick right at his head," I said.

"Now I wish I coulda seen that." Benny smiled. "Whatever you do, don't let him get near us. Stenkevitz ain't never been right in the head."

"I won't," I said.

"Who are you talking to?" Stenkevitz demanded. "Your spy buddies? I hear you. Don't think I don't!" Stenkevitz's head bobbed forward, and I thought for a moment he had passed out. Then he lifted his head, shaking it from side to side.

"Who are you? What are you doin' out here?" he asked. His tone was different now, confused, like he'd just woken up from a nap.

"I told you. We were on the ship."

"What ship?"

"The one that exploded and sank. The USS *Indianapolis*," I said.

"What? The *Indy* didn't explode, it's right down there," he said. He pointed underwater.

"Uh. Sure. It's down there because it sank; everybody said it got torpedoed," I said.

"What are you talking about?" he asked, perplexed. "It's right there. Right under the water. It's perfectly fine. I'm going to the gedunk to get some ice cream. They got some good ice cream there. I like chocolate myself. Why haven't I seen you on the ship before?"

I didn't know what to say. Just moments ago, he'd been a raving maniac. If I said the wrong thing, I could set him off again.

"You got anything to eat?" he asked.

I shook my head.

His head bobbed forward again, and for several minutes he didn't say anything. I thought for a moment I even heard him snoring. I tried to quietly paddle our raft away from him, but I must have splashed too loudly because he jerked awake.

"Who are you? Where did you come from?"

"I told you, my name is Patri—"

"You got any food?"

Benny's eyes fluttered open. "He still here?"

"Yeah," I muttered.

"I'm going to board your ship and search it!" Stenkevitz said. "I'm a sergeant in the United States Marine Corps, and I believe you're carrying contraband. Prepare to be boarded!"

"You still got your stick with the nail, pipsqueak?" Benny asked. I looked at him with alarm. I'd just told him I'd thrown the stick at Stenkevitz and he'd forgotten. Or maybe I hadn't told him. I couldn't remember anymore. The sun dazzled my eyes and I started to wonder if I was hallucinating. Was Stenkevitz really there? Was I dreaming all of this? Why couldn't I wake up and be back in my bunk on Guam?

A wave jostled the pallet and brought me back to the present. I wasn't dreaming. Everything that happened was real.

"Nope. I don't have that stick anymore," I said. "I tossed it at him and hit him in the head. Made him drop the gun," I said.

Benny chuckled. "Now I'da given a week's pay to have seen that. But listen, you can't let him get close.

Or most of all, let him get on the raft. That tub o' lard will capsize us for sure."

While we were talking, Stenkevitz was splashing and paddling in the water, and had cut the distance to the raft in half. He was making a lot of noise with all of his shouting and thrashing about. So much that he hadn't noticed that several yards behind him, a dorsal fin had broken the water's surface.

It cut through the water like a knife.

And it was headed straight for him.

"I don't think that's going to be a problem, Benny," I said.

CHAPTER FIFTEEN

RUCKUS

★ ★ ★

'm going to board your ship and seize your stores. This is wartime. I got rights to search an enemy vessel," he said.

"Look out!" I shouted. "There's a sha—"

I didn't even get the word out of my mouth before, as Benny would say, "he lost his flippin' mind."

"Shark! No! Don't! No! Sharks . . . Stop . . . Don't let it get me!" His sunken eyes grew wide and he spun his head around, looking everywhere for the shark. It was closing fast.

"It's behind you," I said. "Don't move. Stop splashing. I think any kind of noise or splashing makes them attack."

"No! No! No!" he cried. He thrashed and shrieked in the water. The shark was speeding up.

"You've got to calm down!" I said, but my voice had no volume, and I don't think he heard me.

The shark smacked into one of the corpses, and the impact rocked the whole group. The body rose up out of the water, and the great fish bit off the dead man's arm at the elbow. It had gotten what it came for, and it sunk below the water.

Stenkevitz was weeping. Now he'd floated past us, and I looked around to see if there was anything I could toss to him that might help him defend himself. My stick with the nail was nowhere in sight.

And unfortunately for the sergeant, it looked like the giant predator wanted a second helping. It surfaced again, this time in front of Stenkevitz. He went completely nuts, ranting as it circled him slowly.

"Get away from me!" he screamed, spinning and thrashing uncontrollably. "Stay away!"

If I didn't know better, I'd have thought the shark was toying with him. Like it enjoyed making him crazy. Stenkevitz followed it with his eyes. His screams turned to frightened moans.

"What you goin' to do, sport?" Benny whispered.

"I don't know," I said. "Nothing? He was going to board—"

"You're the captain of this ship. You got a fellow crewman in the water in a state of distress. Stenkevitz might be a dunderhead, but he's a fellow marine. What have I told you about marines?" he rasped.

"They leave no man behind," I said.

"That's right." Benny coughed and it sounded like a hollow drum was beating deep in his lungs. Part of me was amazed that he was still alive.

"I don't know what to do. He's drifting away, and I don't really want to leave him behind, Benny, honest I don't. But I'm not strong enough to paddle the raft to him," I said as I slapped my hand down on the pallet. "It may not weigh much now that it's coming apart—" Stopping midsentence, I turned around and felt the boards one by one. The pallet was fastened together in a crisscross pattern. Four thick boards made up the foundation and two-inch wide planks were nailed to each side of them. One of the corner planks had come loose where the sharks had bitten through it. I carefully rose to my hands and knees. Putting one knee on the plank, I pulled at it with all the strength I had left.

I glanced over at Stenkevitz. He moaned like Teddy did. But the shark didn't care. It burst forward and tore into the corpse on his left.

"Stop! Someone help me! Please!" Stenkevitz was wailing like a drowning cat.

I groaned with the effort and pulled on the plank. It still wouldn't give.

"C'mon, champ," Benny said. "Put your back into it. You got a marine pinned down. He's takin' enemy fire. And he's waitin' on you to come to his aid. Stenkevitz might be a sorry excuse for a human bein', but when the chips are down all that matters is that globe and anchor on his collar. You gotta help him."

I grunted with the strain. "I'm trying," I said through gritted teeth. The wood splintered and cracked. A big piece of it came loose in my hands. It was about three feet long, blunt on one end, with a sharp point on the other.

The shark ripped several grisly bites from the corpse, and now it was circling again.

"Hey! Stenkevitz! Heads up!" I said. I tossed the board. It whirled through the air and landed about five or six feet in front of him. He understood immediately and paddled his way toward it, snatching it up in his hands.

"Did he reach it?" Benny asked.

"Yeah. He got it," I said.

When the shark attacked again, Stenkevitz clubbed and poked at it like a man possessed. The shark shook and thrashed, kicking up the waves. Stenkevitz was floating away from us, the distance growing the longer they struggled.

"Try to whack it in the gills," I shouted. But my voice was merely a weak rasp.

The confrontation with Stenkevitz and the effort to break off the board had taken all the energy I had left. I lay back down on the raft. My head felt funny and the sky was spinning. I closed my eyes. Somewhere off in the distance I could still hear Stenkevitz shouting and cursing at the shark, but eventually I drifted off to sleep.

I woke up as the sun was sinking in the western sky. The waters were calm, and an eerie silence blanketed everything for miles around. My muscles were cramped. I could barely move or see. I struggled to a sitting position. It felt like I'd been staring at a light bulb for hours. When the spots in front of my eyes finally cleared, I looked around in every direction.

Stenkevitz was nowhere to be seen.

CHAPTER SIXTEEN

FAITH

★ ★ ★

As the morning stretched into the afternoon, we baked in the sun. My face was blistered and burning. I pulled my shirt off and wrapped it over my head like a scarf. If I was ever more tired in my life, I didn't remember when.

We dozed in the sweltering heat. There was nothing else to do. I started thinking about Mom and Dad. I hated to think it, but it might be better if they were dead. If they were alive, they would never know what happened to their sons. We weren't going to be rescued. Maybe they'd find out that we survived the war on Guam. That would be the first place they would look for us. And I'm sure they'd find Sister Mary Teresa. But we hadn't even told her what our plans were. As far as she knew, we disappeared from the orphanage and never came back. I felt bad about that. But if we had told her what we were planning, she would have tried to stop us. Mom and Dad would just be left with a lifetime of wondering.

Me and Teddy would die out here, and Mom and Dad would spend the rest of their lives never knowing what happened to us. I probably should have left a note somewhere for someone to find after the *Indianapolis* departed. That way they would know why I did what I did. At least they'd understand that I was trying to find them. To bring us all back together.

As I slept, I dreamed strange and unusual dreams. There were ships sailing all around us. The three of us could stand, and we had our voices back and we were no longer dying of thirst. But no matter how loud we yelled, or whatever noise we made, no one could hear or see us. We waved our shirts, tried everything we could think of to get their attention, but they just sailed past us.

I dreamed of strange metal insects flying in the sky, buzzing in the air above. Their wings and tails glinted in the sunlight. One of them dipped low and flew right over us. I wanted to reach out and pluck it from the sky, because it looked like it was going to land on the water. *Watch out, little metal bug!* I thought. *These waters are full of sharks!* I watched it until it disappeared from sight.

Right before twilight, we floated into another large debris field filled with bodies and flotsam from the wreck. More sharks than I could count picked their way through the wreckage on the hunt for an easy meal. To make it worse, we were all dying of thirst. Teddy woke up just as the sun went down. The raft was bobbing in the waves again. He dipped his hand in the salt water and put it to his lips.

"You can't let him be drinkin' that water, pip-squeak," Benny said. His voice was getting weaker.

"Teddy! Stop!" I said. But he didn't listen. He gulped down a big mouthful of seawater. A few seconds later he threw it all back up. It didn't stop him. He put another handful to his mouth.

"Patty boy, you gotta make him quit," he said. "He drinks much more of it, he's gonna get sicker and eventually it'll kill him."

"Teddy! Don't drink that water!" I yelled at him again, but he wouldn't look at me.

The raft was barely keeping us afloat anymore. It kept sinking below the surface. But it still rocked to and fro, as I slowly crawled toward Teddy, groaning with each movement. I reached up and yanked his hand away from his mouth.

"Aah!" Teddy said. He took a swing at me, his fist connecting with the side of my head.

"Ow! Teddy, calm down!" I yelled.

My brother wasn't listening. He plunged both hands into the water and lifted them to his mouth, drinking deeply. I knocked his hands aside, and he lunged at me. He was mad with thirst. It gave him an extra dose of strength. Even though he was two years younger, Teddy was almost my size. He was a solid kid and probably as strong as I am. I tended to forget that because he was fragile in so many other ways.

I scrambled back up and pushed him over. He flopped onto his back.

"Stop it right now, Teddy! Right now!" I had very little voice left.

He kicked me in the chest. I grabbed his foot and held on as tight as I could. He shook and thrashed, trying to get free. His foot was wet and slippery. I just couldn't hold on, and he jerked it free. "Aah!" he cried. All of our wrestling around was causing the pallet to splash and rock in the water.

"Look sharp, kid," Benny called.

The largest shark we'd seen yet lunged out of the water and landed on the raft right next to me. I felt its teeth graze my leg and its jaws snapped shut. I screamed and twirled away, slipping off the pallet and into the ocean. As I tumbled over and over in the water, Benny shouted, "Watch behind you!"

I turned to see the shark coming straight at me. There was no time to do anything but kick at its nose. The rough skin cut the bottoms of my feet. I could feel it brush against my side as it dove below me. When I spun back around, I found that the pallet had come completely apart. The largest remaining chunk was keeping Teddy and Benny afloat. The rest of it was mostly splinters, but one small corner section was still bobbing just below the surface. I grabbed it, clutching it to my chest. The boards held me up a little if I kicked my legs.

"You okay, pipsqueak?" Benny said.

"I got bit, Benny," I said. "It hurts. I'm bleeding."

"No time for pain or blood, skipper. You got another shark at nine o'clock!" I couldn't figure it out at first, but something had happened to Benny's voice. It seemed stronger and clearer. But I didn't have time to consider it. The shark had resurfaced, and it lunged straight for me. I screamed as loud as I could and smashed the chunk of pallet down on its head. This one looked about the size of a battleship. Why did the biggest, relentless, and most aggressive ones come out at night?

Battleship thrashed and slapped its tail on the water. I kept yelling and smashing the pallet against its head. The water around us was a flurry of kicks and flashing teeth.

"C'mon!" I shouted. "You want more? C'mon! Keep coming at me!" I unleashed a string of words that would have gravely disappointed Sister Mary Teresa.

"Pipsqueak! Patty boy! It's gone! Stop! Save your strength. It's going to be a long night." I didn't listen. I was sick of everything. Sick of waiting for a rescue that was never coming. Sick to death of the ocean. I wanted to kill every single shark in it with my bare hands.

"Shut up, Benny! Shut up! I'm done listening to you! Done! Do you hear me? We're going to die out here. Our raft is gone. We have no water! No food! NOTHING! Just shut up!"

"You really think there ain't nobody comin' to rescue you, champ?" he said.

"No! No one is coming! Just stop talking about it!"

"Then what do you call that?" He pointed over my shoulder with his burned, gnarled hand.

I looked behind me. Piercing the inky blackness of the night was a bright white column of light.

A spotlight from a ship pointing straight up into the heavens above.

CHAPTER SEVENTEEN

LOST AT SEA

★ ★ ★

The ship was miles away from us. But the light was so clear in the darkness it felt like we could reach right out and touch it. A plane appeared in the sky, circling the column of light, and we could see the crew dropping supplies into the ocean.

"What if they don't see us?" I said. Teddy and Benny were floating on the broken piece of the pallet. I held on to it with one hand and kept one of the broken boards I'd smashed on the shark in the other. We could only stay afloat with a few kicks of our legs. Of course, each kick sent more blood pouring into the water from the gash in my leg.

"You don't gotta worry, pipsqueak. Them swabbies is going to do what's called a grid search. That's standard operatin' procedure when a ship goes down. They'll blanket the whole area lookin' for crew. All you gotta do is hold on and they'll find you," Benny said.

As if on cue, Battleship returned. It burst out of the water right next to me, so sudden that I screamed in surprise. Out of instinct, I swung the board in my hand as hard as I could and it connected, striking the giant beast in the gills. Battleship swam away from me. *The bigger they come, the harder they'll fall*, I told myself. *Especially once I'm through with them.*

"Keep an eye out, Patty boy," Benny said. "It's around here somewhere."

"*You think so?*" I said with an angry snarl.

It was hard to concentrate. I kept wishing the spotlight was closer so I could see, or better yet, that someone on that plane or the ship would spot us.

"Aah! Aah!" Teddy suddenly wailed. He pointed behind me. I spun quickly in the water. Battleship was back. I couldn't help but think how its dorsal fin was like the periscope on a submarine. It was tracking us through the water like the Japanese sub must have tracked the *Indianapolis* that night.

I started to cry. I couldn't help it. Safety seemed so far away. As the shark crossed the water toward me, I was almost ready to give up. It passed me slowly, back and forth, biding its time. I didn't want to cry. I wanted to believe Benny. I wanted to trust that the navy would find us. But I was so tired.

"Buck up, Patty boy. You gonna let a fish beat you? Would that bum Greenberg, who by the way should not even stand in the same room as the Iron Horse, give up? No. He would not. Now you tell yourself you ain't going to let that shark win. And you are going to save your brother."

"Stop telling me to buck up," I shouted. "You buck up! I'm tired of you telling me everything is going to be okay! It's not going to be okay. That ship and that plane probably won't even see us. I hate you and I hate the Japanese and I hate my mom and dad for putting us on that plane in the first place! Why did they—"

"Don't you even say it!" Benny roared back. "You wanna pop off at me, you go right ahead. You wanna give Teddy a smack in the bean, you go right ahead. That's what brothers do. But you don't *ever* get to

question your mom and pops, who had to do the hard-
est thing they ever imagined in their whole entire
lives, which was to put you two buckos on that plane.
You think they didn't know there wasn't no time till
the invasion happened? You don't believe your mother
sank to the ground and cried like a baby as she watched
that plane take off with you on it? You got yourself
some world-class parents, kid. They might have given
up their lives to save yours. I know how you seen these
scars on my back. Well let me tell you, I didn't get all
of 'em from teachin' Tojo the consequences of sucker-
punchin' the United States of America. Most of 'em
come courtesy of my old man, who never met a beatin'
he didn't like. My pops was a vicious drunk. You
wanna know what I got when I spilled a glass a water
on the floor of our rathole apartment in the Bronx? I
got the belt. I didn't get no trip to Yankee Stadium or
tea and biscuits at Macy's. Sometimes when he was all
worked up, he used my mom as a punchin' bag. And
when I tried to stop him, when I weren't much bigger
than you? He liked to put his cigar out on my back.
So anytime you wanna compare who got the better

deal when it comes to parents, you just say the word. Now you are goin' to wipe your eyes and straighten up. And you *will* get found by them swabbies. Are we clear?"

Off in the distance, the searchlight teased me. I was tired of talking. Tired of living. Maybe Benny was right. Maybe he wasn't. Maybe he'd had a hard life. But in case he hadn't noticed, my life hadn't been a walk in the park lately. So he could keep his big fat trap shut.

As the night grew long, the waves grew bigger. And they were carrying us away from the searchlight. I wondered if the navy was picking up the rest of the crew right now. I remembered the large group of men who were floating in the water that first night. Had they survived? Had the sharks—

"AAH! AAH!" Teddy shouted. I knew from the frightened expression on his face that the shark was probably creeping up behind me. I didn't need to look back and see it. And I knew then that I was done. There was no more fight left in me. Exhaustion washed over me as I let go of the hunk of pallet that was keeping

Benny and Teddy afloat. Slowly, I started to sink into the water.

"Benny, Teddy . . . I'm sorry," I said. "So sorry . . ."

Behind me, the shark thrashed its tail as it sliced through the water. It was nearly upon me. I closed my eyes. For the first time in a long time, I felt at peace.

A bright light cut through the darkness and the sharp, cracking report of rifle shots startled me and my eyes flew open. Two, then three shots in quick succession, then a half a dozen more. I kicked my legs and rose in the water, turning in time to see that big battleship of a shark explode into a million little pieces. A searchlight swept over the water and settled its beam on us.

And out of the blackest night, a large ship appeared.

CHAPTER EIGHTEEN

THE REST

★ ★ ★

The admiral stayed by my bedside until he realized I wasn't going to talk to him.

"Why won't you answer me?" he asked with a frustrated sigh. When I didn't say anything, he put his hat on and turned to the doctor on duty. "Waste of my time! Have someone call me when he's feeling better, but not before. You make him understand he *is* going to talk." He stalked out of the hospital room with the doctor at his heels.

But he didn't realize that my health had nothing to do with it. My answers were my own. What happened out there belonged to Benny, Teddy, and me. I'd heard that a little over three hundred men survived the wreck. There were over 1,100 crewmen on the *Indianapolis* when it left Guam. Some had died when the ship blew up, but about six hundred died in the water. Only three hundred and seventeen survived. All of us who were out there—we were going to be forever changed by it. And we don't have to answer anyone's questions unless it's our choice. Those answers belong to us and no one else.

When the ship finally reached us, the sailors pulled us out of the water. They lowered nets over the side and sent men down to carry us up. Marines patrolling the deck with rifles kept the sharks off us. Teddy and I were hustled to the infirmary. My leg wound took over forty stitches to close. I lost track of what happened to Benny. It took the sailors and the ship's captain a while to figure out that we weren't part of the crew. But no one really asked us what we were doing out there or how we even got on the *Indianapolis* in the first place. They just fed us chicken broth and tried to get us cleaned up. The only way they could get the diesel fuel off our skin was to scrub us down with kerosene. I drank so much water they told me to slow down before I got sick. But I got sick anyway.

Several times. I asked for Benny, but no one seemed to know what I was talking about.

Then I fell asleep, and I didn't remember waking up until I was settled in the hospital here in Leyte, with Teddy sleeping in the bed across from me. At first I worried I was dreaming. If I wasn't careful, I'd wake up back in the water with a dozen sharks bearing down on me. But every time I woke up I was still in a bed with clean sheets and cups of applesauce and plenty of water.

Once, I jerked awake as Nurse Anderson was changing the bandage on my leg.

"Where am I?" I asked her. My throat and mouth were still raw and covered with sores and blisters. Every part of me ached.

"You're in Leyte, hon," she said. "You've had quite an ordeal. You need to rest."

"Where's Benny?"

"Who's Benny, dear?" she asked.

"Benjamin Franklin Poindexter, Private First Class, United States Marine Corps. He was with us on the raft. He was rescued with us. He has to be here somewhere."

"I'm afraid I don't know anything about that, dear," she said.

I wanted to ask her more questions, but my eyes wouldn't stay open. The next time I woke up, a man was sitting in a wheelchair next to my bedside. It took me a moment to recognize Sergeant Stenkevitz. His face was sunburned, blistered, and covered in cuts and bruises.

"Hey, kid," he said.

I didn't say anything.

"I . . . uh . . . you doing okay? They treating you all right in here?" he asked.

If I said something . . . anything . . . I worried I might get Benny in trouble. So I just stared at him.

"I . . . uh . . . remember some of what happened out there. Like when I came across you and your brother in the ocean. It was . . . I was . . . a little crazy, I'll admit. Me and three other guys got separated from our group out there. They all died; the sharks got them. And I guess I lost it a little bit. What I'm saying is, I'm sorry. It was just . . . I didn't know what I . . . I'm sorry," he said, and bowed his head.

Realizing I wasn't going to say anything, he finally turned his wheelchair and headed for the door. But I couldn't let him go. I didn't know what to say to him, how to forgive him for what he'd done. But there was something I had to ask him.

"Sergeant?" I asked.

He spun the chair around to face me.

"Yeah, kid?"

"No one will tell me where Benny is. Do you know?"

"Who?"

"Benny. He . . . uh . . . he was with us on the raft. When you found us."

"You mean Benny Poindexter?"

"Yes."

Sergeant Stenkevitz's face took on an ashen look. For a long minute he was quiet. I could tell there was something he needed to tell me, but he didn't want to say it.

"Kid, I . . . uh . . . I don't know how to say this, but Benny wasn't with you."

"What? Yes he was!"

"No, he wasn't."

"How do you know?"

He paused a minute, thinking. A look of understanding came over him.

"He snuck you aboard, didn't he? You were hiding in that crate! I knew he was up to something. I thought he might be smuggling liquor or cigarettes. But it was you? Why?"

I still wouldn't give Benny up.

"Where is he?" I took a more demanding tone.

"Listen, son . . ."

"I'm not your son! Benny was out there with us on the raft! He was rescued with us, I swear. Now somebody better tell me where he is!"

Stenkevitz shook his head. "He wasn't there."

"What do you mean?"

"I mean he wasn't there. I . . . He was with me in the brig. When the . . . he didn't make it off the ship."

I stared at him in disbelief. His words made no sense to me.

"What you mean he didn't make it? He was there with us the whole time! I gave him water when I still had the canteen. I listened to every one of his instructions. He told me jokes. Stories about his life. And he made me promise not to die! Benjamin Franklin Poindexter, Private First Class, United States Marine Corps—"

"He went down with the ship."

He might as well have punched me in the gut. Nothing was making sense.

"No! You're lying! He came back for us . . . he . . . He told us to wait for him in the hold, and if he didn't come back, to make our way topside. But he did come back. He did!"

Stenkevitz shook his head.

"He came tearing out of the hold right after I did," he said. "Right when the ship first got hit. We were headed topside when we heard somebody calling for help from the brig. It was on fire. Smoke so thick you could barely see. Benny was lifting debris off an injured sailor, when a steam pipe exploded. The fitting blew off right next to his face. He was burned up pretty good. Still, he kept trying to help. A section of the pipe landed on top of one of the guys, and it was hot. He burned his hands real bad trying to get it off the guy. But he just kept going, pulling burning rubble off of those injured men. The fire was spreading, but we got three crewmen out. Then the ship listed and whole bunch of debris fell directly on him. Me and the others tried to get him loose. We did. But the fire just got too close, and we couldn't free him. He screamed at us to get out. To save ourselves. We tried using a fire hose to beat back the flames, but we had no water pressure."

"No . . . you . . . you're lying . . ."

He shook his head. "I'm sorry. Benny was a pain in my backside and he cheated at poker. But he was one brave son of a gun. He *ordered* us to leave him. He saved us."

"No! You left him behind! You don't know what happened after that. Maybe he got loose and came to the hold—"

"I know it's hard, kid. We lost so many good men. But he never made it to the hold. I know it for a fact."

"How do you know?!" I was getting angry, gripping my metal cup of applesauce with both hands.

Stenkevitz bowed his head. When he looked up he had tears in his eyes.

"Because I dogged the hatch. I dogged the hatch. Benny told me to seal him up to help save the ship. He kept yelling at me to do it. I'm sorry. God forgive me. I'm so sorry."

"NO! NO!" I threw my cup of applesauce at Stenkevitz. He winced. It missed him by a foot and clattered against the wall behind him. Applesauce spattered everywhere.

"I'm sorry—"

"GET OUT! YOU GET OUT!" I shouted. Nurse Anderson burst into the room.

"What's going on?!" she asked.

"It's my fault," Stenkevitz said. "I was just leaving." He slowly wheeled his way out of the room. Teddy had woken up and was staring at me with big eyes. I started crying.

Nurse Anderson came to my bedside.

"What's wrong?" she asked.

"Please, just leave me alone," I said. I turned away from her toward the wall. My body trembled, wracked with sobs, and once I opened the floodgates, I couldn't stop. Stenkevitz was lying. Benny had been there. He'd made sure we were safe. But he hadn't gone down with the ship. I know. He was there with us the whole time. He *was* there.

Why wouldn't anyone tell me where he was now?

Then I felt guilty. What if I hadn't saved him? What if he'd slipped into the water or been taken by a shark right before the navy found us? By the time they pulled us aboard, I'd lost track of everything. I'd been so tired. My last words to him were full of anger. He couldn't be gone. He just couldn't.

I closed my eyes, trying to stop the tears. And I must have drifted off to sleep. I woke up to the sound of excited voices coming from the hallway outside our room. I wondered for a moment if the admiral had come back to demand his answers. But the voices somehow pulled at my memory. I sat up to listen, concentrating.

When they stepped into the room, I didn't recognize them at first. They looked so different from what I remembered. The man had crutches and walked like his legs had been broken, but never healed properly. The woman's hair had been shorn almost to her scalp. She was skeletally thin. But when she saw me, she smiled.

"Patrick?" she said.

"Mom? Dad?" Then they were rushing at me. I leapt out of the bed and waddled on my wounded feet toward them. We met in the middle of the room and I thought we would crush each other with our hugs.

"My God, Patrick," Dad said. "I never thought we would see you again. I nev—" Overcome with emotion, he couldn't speak anymore. Tears spilled down his cheeks.

Mom leaned back and took my arms in her hands. Her lips were cracked and swollen. She was stooped, and her shoulders slumped like she was in pain. I had no idea what had happened to them, what they had endured. Whatever it was, it must have been horrible. But none of that mattered now.

"I did it, Mom," I said, feeling an enormous invisible weight lifting off me. "I did what you asked. I took care of Teddy. Just like I promised."

"Oh, honey," she said, hugging me again. "I know you did. You did more than anyone could have asked."

But I couldn't stop. "He's okay, Mom. I mean he hasn't talked—won't talk—since we left you, but he's alive. And all through the war on Guam, and then when the ship blew up, I kept him alive. Me and Benny kept him alive."

"Who's Benny, dear?" Mom asked me.

"Don't worry, Mom," I said. "I tell you all about him. About everything."

We were quiet then. And for the first time, I realized it didn't matter if what Stenkevitz said was true or not. Benny had been there with us the whole time. He kept us alive. He saved us. No matter what anyone said. Dogged hatch or no, Benny Poindexter, Private First Class, United States Marine Corps did as he promised. He got us back to our parents.

Mom and Dad were both crying now. Their sobs finally roused Teddy from his coma-like sleep. He burrowed out from under the pile of sheets and sat up in his bed, looking at us and blinking several times. His eyes narrowed in confusion, but it didn't take him long to understand what he was seeing.

"Mama?" he said.

AFTERWORD

First commissioned on November 15, 1932, the USS *Indianapolis* was a Portland-class heavy cruiser named after the capital city of Indiana. It had a distinguished service record. Before World War II, it carried President Franklin D. Roosevelt on several excursions, including a goodwill tour of South America in 1936. And during the war, it served as a flagship of the admiral of the United States Fifth Fleet until it sank on July 30, 1945.

The USS *Indianapolis* began its final, fateful voyage on July 16, 1945, when it departed San Francisco. It was on a top secret mission. In its hold it carried components to complete the first atomic bomb. The *Indy* sailed from San Francisco to Hawaii, and after refueling, departed for the island of Tinian, where it would deliver its cargo. The famed B-29 bomber *Enola Gay* waited at the US air base on Tinian. On August 6, 1945, the *Enola Gay* would drop the atomic bomb on the Japanese city of Hiroshima, signaling the beginning of the end of the Japanese Empire.

The *Indy*'s captain, Charles Butler McVay, came from a long line of distinguished naval officers. The cruiser had undergone extensive repairs in San Francisco, and Captain McVay used the voyage to test the engines and prepare for the ship's next mission. Having made its delivery at Tinian, the *Indy* sailed for Guam. There it took on a number of new crewmen, and on July 28, 1945, departed for the Leyte Gulf in the Philippines, where it was to rendezvous with the battleship USS *Idaho*. Should Japan refuse to surrender, the final attack on the island of Japan was scheduled to launch from the Philippines, and the *Indianapolis* would be a part of the invasion fleet.

At fourteen minutes past midnight on July 30, 1945, the *Indianapolis* was struck amidships by two Type 95 torpedoes launched from the Japanese submarine *I-58*, captained by Lieutenant Commander Mochitsura Hashimoto. The torpedoes could not have been more perfectly placed. They hit the *Indianapolis* on its starboard side, striking a fuel tank and powder magazine. The resulting explosion ripped a gaping hole in the hull. The heat from the ensuing fire caused huge sections of the steel deck to melt, as well as several deaths by asphyxiation.

All shipwide communication and electricity was knocked out immediately on impact. Because no one was able to tell the engine room to shut off the engines, the *Indianapolis* traveled over a mile farther, taking in massive amounts of seawater through the hull breach. The ship rolled to its starboard side and sank in under twelve minutes.

There were 1,196 crewmen aboard the ship. Of that number, roughly 300 were killed in the explosion. Approximately 900 men abandoned ship and made it into the water. Despite the enormity of the catastrophe, most of the survivors expected to be rescued sometime the next day. In fact, a distress call was sent out and received by at least three different naval stations. However, wartime protocol required the ship to send at least two distinct signals—otherwise the navy assumed a single signal was a Japanese trick to lure ships into an ambush. The *Indianapolis* was so gravely damaged and sank so quickly that there was no time for the second message to go out.

The crewmen's luck took another horrible turn in the early morning hours, when sharks began feeding on the survivors. For the next three and a half days, the men of the *Indianapolis* endured what scientists have called the worst encounter between humans and sharks in history. The path the *Indianapolis* was taking to the Philippines took them through some of the most heavily populated shark habitats in the world. Many of the men were weak or wounded, and were unable to fend off the nearly constant feeding of the sharks.

Of the roughly 900 men who abandoned the sinking cruiser, only 317 ultimately survived. On August 2, 1945, Lieutenant (jg) Wilbur C. Gwinn was piloting his PV-1 Ventura bomber on a routine patrol when he spotted a group of men in the water. He radioed his coordinates to the air base in Peleliu, and another pilot, Lieutenant R. Adrian Marks, was sent to investigate in a PBY seaplane. On his way to the site, Marks spotted the destroyer USS *Cecil Doyle* and reported to its captain that he was en route to find survivors of a possible shipwreck. Under his own authority, the captain of the *Cecil Doyle* turned his ship and headed toward the site at top speed.

When Marks arrived over the area, he witnessed several of the *Indy*'s crewmen under attack by sharks. Disobeying orders, Marks landed his plane on the ocean surface and taxied to pick up individual survivors. When the plane's cabin was full, he tied men to the wings and fuselage with parachute cord. In all, Lieutenant Marks pulled over fifty men from the water.

That night, the USS *Doyle* arrived on the scene and again, going against standard protocol, the *Doyle*'s captain turned the ship's biggest searchlight directly up into the sky to act as a beacon for other ships. More of them arrived throughout the night, and the remaining crew of the USS *Indianapolis* was finally saved.

It was the worst disaster at sea in US naval history. After their rescue, the crew was taken to a naval hospital on Leyte. The Japanese surrendered on August 15, 1945. The war was over.

The navy court-martialed Captain McVay, much to the dismay of his surviving crew. This decision shocked most ship commanders of the era. In an unprecedented move, the navy called Commander Hashimoto to testify against McVay. Captain McVay was convicted of "hazarding his ship by failing to zig-zag," a technique used by ships to avoid submarines. This, despite Commander Hashimoto's testimony that zigzagging would not have prevented him from sinking the USS *Indianapolis*. The court-martial also failed to consider that Captain McVay's orders were for him to zigzag at his discretion, visibility permitting.

Captain McVay accepted his punishment stoically, in the highest traditions of a naval officer. He was the only ship commander who served in World War II to be court-martialed after losing his ship in combat. Despite overwhelming evidence that the navy itself had placed the ship in harm's way—naval records show that naval command knew submarines were in the area and denied Captain McVay's request for a destroyer escort—the conviction was upheld and even-tually ruined McVay's career. He retired from the navy in 1949. Despite the unwavering support of his surviving crew, McVay received angry letters from the families of those who died in the accident for years afterward. Guilt exacted its toll, and in 1968 Captain McVay took his own life.

But the story of the USS *Indianapolis* does not end there. In the late 1990s a twelve-year-old boy named Hunter Scott took up McVay's cause as part of a history project. His interviews with *Indianapolis* survivors and review of hundreds of documents concerning the shipwreck led him and many of those survivors to testify before Congress. In 2000, Congress passed a resolution, signed by President Clinton, that exonerated Captain McVay from any fault in the sinking of the USS *Indianapolis*.

At last the great ship and her captain could rest.

SOURCES

Kurzman, Dan. *Fatal Voyage: The Sinking of the USS* Indianapolis. New York: Crown Publishing Group, 1990.

Newcomb, Richard F. *Abandon Ship!: The Saga of the U.S.S.* Indianapolis, *the Navy's Greatest Sea Disaster.* New York: HarperCollins, 1960.

Stanton, Doug. *In Harm's Way: The Sinking of the U.S.S.* Indianapolis *and the Extraordinary Story of Its Survivors.* London: Macmillan Publishers, 2001.

www.ussindianapolis.org

ACKNOWLEDGMENTS

This book, while based on a real event, is a work of fiction. With the exception of historical figures, such as Captain McVay, all other characters are not based on real persons. I would like to thank Christopher Moore, Flip Nicklin, and Roland Smith for their help and input into this project. Dr. Sonny Berger deserves special thanks for his time and patience with my innumerable questions on sharks and shark behavior. Any mistakes in the book are purely my own.

Thanks also to the team at Scholastic for their encouragement and unwavering support. My editor, Jenne Abramowitz, for her spot-on suggestions; Abby McAden for her belief in me as a writer, not to mention our many years of friendship; and to Jana Haussmann, Ed Masessa, and Robin Hoffman and everyone at Scholastic Book Fairs for getting my books in front of so many readers. The entire Scholastic sales, editorial, marketing, and publicity teams have been a delight to work with. I know from experience how many dedicated people are involved in getting a book onto the shelves and I sincerely thank them all.

At Team Spradlin, thanks to my agent Steven Chudney and to Emily Cotler and my crack website team at Wax Creative. And last, but never least, my family, who puts up with my writer's brain and gracefully endures long periods of me staring off into space while I'm thinking about characters and stories. My son, Mick, and daughter-in-law, Jessica, are the best beta readers anyone could ask for. Thanks to my daughter, Rachel, who is an inspiration to everyone, but especially me. And I would be nowhere without my wife, Kelly, who does everything, but most of all never falters in her belief in me. Every man should be so lucky.

"Hero" is a word that can often be loosely applied to many. For the captain and crew of the USS *Indianapolis* the word does not do them justice. They were and are beyond heroic. Their story is an example of courage, grace, and determination unmatched. They earned and deserve our thanks. They certainly have mine.

INTO THE KILLING SEAS: A CONVERSATION WITH AUTHOR MICHAEL P. SPRADLIN

Q: *Into the Killing Seas* is based on a harrowing true event from World War II, but Patrick and Teddy's story is purely fictional. What kinds of research did you do to ensure that their journey was a believable one?

A: I started by reading everything I could find on the tragedy, including survivors' accounts of the ordeal. I reviewed hundreds of navy documents on the incident, everything from after-action reports to photos of the survivors in the aftermath. Since this was the worst disaster at sea in US naval history, a lot has been written on the fate of the USS *Indianapolis*. There are a great number of primary sources to draw from.

This story is set in World War II, which means I had a treasure trove of photos, records, and official documents to utilize. Previously, I'd written a series of books set in the Middle Ages, and the research for that was much more difficult. I had to rely on translations, paintings, and tapestries, and it was hard to know what information was accurate and what was not. With this story, I not only had actual documented material to work with but also video and audio recordings. These were extremely helpful in developing characters. Reading books and watching movies written and filmed during this period was an excellent way to pick up the rhythm and diction of speech during the war years. Spoken language, slang, and even the manner people engage in conversation changes over time, and I wanted my characters to sound like they would have in the 1940s.

Benny Poindexter is a perfect example of this. My model for him was Jimmy Cagney, a famous actor from the thirties and forties. He specialized in tough guy roles, and in most of his films he spoke with a rapid-fire delivery and a slightly off-kilter vocabulary. I wanted Benny to sound like him and share a lot of his physical characteristics. He certainly has his tough guy attitude. Yet inside he's a complete softy. I see Benny as a man of his time. Those men and woman have been called the Greatest Generation, and I'm not certain that the term does them justice. Like many of those men, Benny possesses native—but not necessarily academic—intelligence. He's street-smart. Yet he's more intelligent than most anyone else we meet in the book. He has an innate understanding of people and of right and wrong. Like his contemporaries, he's endured hardships and solved problems that I'm not sure many of us could handle today. When you talk about World War II you have to realize that millions of eighteen- to twenty-year-old men *saved the world*. This is not exaggeration. These men left farms and factories, cities and small towns; they traveled to the far corners of the world to defeat fascism. They did not give up, they endured unimaginable hardships, and they simply refused to accept defeat. And they were *kids*—most of them barely out of high school. We owe them the world we live in today. The men of the USS *Indianapolis* were among the finest examples of the bravery, courage, and sense of duty exhibited by the men and women who served the war effort.

Q: In researching shark behavior, did you learn anything that would be helpful to survive an attack? How do you think you'd fare?

A: I'm pretty sure I'd be dead in about twelve seconds, if not sooner. I have Dr. Sonny Berger of the Bimini Sharklab to thank for most of the shark behavioral information in the book. Contrary to popular belief, sharks do not constantly swim and feed. There are over 400 species of shark, all them with different characteristics. Some of them will only feed every two or three days. But they are opportunistic predators and will eat whatever is close by and looks like food. If a shark attacks you, you should try to remain calm. (Good luck with that!) We've all heard the myth—sharks can smell blood in the water from miles away. But this isn't true. They can smell blood when they are close to it, but it is really noise and vibration that attract sharks. When the USS *Indianapolis* exploded, the sound and vibration traveled through the water like a homing beacon to sharks for miles around.

When you are splashing and thrashing about in the water, you look and sound like a wounded seal or fish, animals that sharks eat. If you keep calm and stop thrashing in the water, you look and sound less like food. If a shark does attack, do not punch them in the face or nose. Their skin is covered with dermal denticles. Essentially these are like teeth on their skin—as if they don't have enough teeth! By cutting and scraping your hands on the dermal denticles, you'll only bleed more, which they *can* smell because they are close enough to touch. This will only excite the shark further. And now you're in real trouble. As a last resort you can poke at the shark's eyes and punch at its gills. There is some evidence that this deters their continued attack. But the best advice, as far as I'm concerned, is to avoid shark-infested waters in the first place!

Q: Patrick has a lot of obstacles to overcome in this book. He has to take care of Teddy when they are separated from their parents, survive the Japanese occupation of Guam, find a way to reunite his family, navigate one of the greatest

disasters in naval history, and keep them alive when the sharks begin to attack. What do you think is the most difficult challenge he faces, and how does he manage to overcome it?

A: I think his most difficult challenge is uncovering the strength he has within himself to carry on. Patrick has to grow up fast. He's one of those people with superhuman determination. He will sacrifice everything to find his parents, which in his mind is how he can save his family, especially Teddy. He is trying to make his family whole again. And on some level, he hopes that reuniting them will perhaps bring Teddy back to himself. I think Patrick manages to overcome his challenges by finding inner strength he doesn't know he has. Some people just seem to possess these untapped reserves when faced with these events. We see it all the time in the news: people survive disasters against incredible odds or become lost in the wilderness for days on end only to emerge relatively unscathed. I firmly believe there are those among us whose brains are wired differently. They're made to handle a crisis. It's like Rudyard Kipling wrote: "If you can keep your head when all about you are losing theirs . . ." Keeping calm in times of great distress can be the difference between life and death. That's Patrick in a nutshell.

Q: At the beginning of the novel, an admiral in the US Navy is trying to get Patrick to describe the events of the sinking of the USS *Indianapolis* and the ensuing shark attacks. Why do you think Patrick is so reluctant to answer his questions?

A: I think there's a multitude of reasons. The first is that Patrick believes by not talking he's protecting Benny. Second, there's the natural survivor's guilt that comes after a tragedy of this magnitude. Patrick learns what happened to the rest of the crew in bits and pieces from the nurses and doctors. The enormity of what occurred weighs on him. I also believe most human beings have a natural reluctance to talk about a tragedy so immense with anyone who doesn't have a similar experience. At this point in the story, I think Patrick is still in shock, and he's not about to do or say anything until he's ready.

Q: How would you describe Patrick's relationship with Benny? Would you say that Benny is his guardian angel?

A: I think readers will each have their own interpretation of Patrick and Benny's relationship, whether Benny's a spirit guide, a father figure, or a guardian angel. However you want to define it, he's there to guide Patrick on his journey. My own interpretation is that, to Patrick, Benny symbolizes strength and courage. He's someone whom Patrick aspires to emulate. I think that's what keeps Patrick going. He wants Benny's approval, without realizing that he already has it.

Q: How did you want readers to react when they discover that Benny died on the ship?

A: I hope their first reaction is a feeling that they've come to the end of a really good story. Then I hope they'll consider the lines between life and death and between this world and the next. What parts of those we love and admire stay with us after they're gone? Do their memories, our love for them, and their love for us still guide us? I believe they do. These are questions novelists far more talented than I have wrestled with for centuries. Benny cared deeply for Patrick and Teddy, and even after he was gone, he still managed to guide them to safety.

Q: Teddy is a damaged character, one who can't fend for himself physically or vocally. Why do you think this is?

A: I think Teddy is just a sensitive soul who is in the worst possible place at the worst possible time. His parents had to make a nearly impossible choice in order to save their children. Obviously he was too young to understand that. The trauma and horrible acts of war he's witnessed on Guam combined with the shipwreck cause him to retreat from interacting with the outside world. He's a symbol of what Patrick could become if he allowed himself. There are many times during the story when Patrick feels himself slipping away. And it's usually his love for Teddy and his family—with a little prodding by Benny—that pulls him back to the mission at hand.

Q: What was it about this period of history that interests you? Why tell this story?

A: I grew up the son of a World War II veteran. It's hard for young readers to understand the impact that World War II had on our society. First, let me say it was nothing short of horrible. Millions of people lost their lives. But in a historical sense, it might be the most transformative event in American history. It completely changed our society. It spurred the beginning of desegregation and women moving into the workplace. The post-war GI Bill allowed many middle-class men from modest backgrounds to attend college. It changed everything.

Growing up, almost every man my father's age that I knew was a veteran of the war. This was an *entire generation* who served. And as I said, they saved the world. And when the war was over, they came back home, set down their duffel bags, and picked up where they had left off. My father, who very rarely spoke of his war experiences, once told me they just did what needed to be done. I find that attitude remarkable. After the war, with the rest of the industrialized world in ashes, the Greatest Generation built a nation on the cutting edge of innovation and technology that became the envy of the world. The war and its aftermath forged modern America in all kinds of ways. Seventy years later we're still living in a world influenced by its outcome. It's fascinating to me to study and learn about it.

Q: In the afterword, you describe the events that followed the crew's rescue. Though Captain Charles McVay doesn't play a part in Patrick and Teddy's story, why did you want to tell readers about his court-martial?

A: I think it's important for readers to know the whole story. And my hope, as always when a reader reads one of my historical novels, is that they'll become interested enough in the period to learn more about it. There is so much to be gained by studying history.

As for Captain McVay, I wanted readers to understand that sometimes you can do everything right, and things still go wrong. Captain McVay was a victim of the system he served and was made a scapegoat by the Navy. He was court-martialed purely as propaganda. The Japanese surrendered shortly after the *Indy* was sunk, and the Navy did not want the loss of those men and their own incompetence brought to light or to have the catastrophe overshadow their great victory. McVay was the only commander of a ship lost in combat during the entire war to be court-martialed. It was a travesty of justice and it eventually caused a good man and an exceptional officer to take his own life.

Q: You're also the author of the series Killer Species. What would you say the difference is between writing historical fiction and purely imagined sci-fi?

A: The differences are not as great as you might imagine. In historical fiction you obviously have to get the facts right, avoid anachronisms, and give the reader a sense of being in the period. But purely imagined science fiction requires research and many of the same rules. I think the most important thing—no matter what genre you're writing in—is to write honestly, write as well as you can, make your story compelling, and try to make your characters relatable to readers.